Breathless

Ross Siblings Book Eight

Breathless

Ross Siblings Book Eight

CHERRIE LYNN

Entangled Publishing, LLC
2614 South Timberline Road
Suite 105, PMB 159
Fort Collins, CO 80525
rights@entangledpublishing.com

Amara is an imprint of Entangled Publishing, LLC.

Edited by Liz Pelletier
Cover design by Fiona Jayde
Cover photography by
GeorgeRudy/iStock
FatSprat/iStock

Manufactured in the United States of America

First Edition November 2018

For Brandon. Thanks for being my rock..

Chapter One

Seth "Ghost" Warren wiped his oil-smudged hands on a well-used rag, frowning into the depths of his 1969 GTO's engine. That should do it. She'd been running hot lately, but he thought he had it pegged to an airflow problem. At least that was what he hoped, since he wasn't too keen on sinking more money into her right now. Frigging thing had been a drain on his finances ever since he'd bought her, but like any good addict, he couldn't stop—at least not when the alternative was selling her. They'd been through too much together.

Thunder rumbled overhead, signaling an afternoon spring thunderstorm and the end of his patience. Sighing, he dropped the hood and gathered his tools, heading toward the garage just as the first fat drops of April rain began to slap the pavement. He could've worked on her under the roof of the garage, but he didn't like the closed-in feel, preferring to tinker with her in the driveway. Until ten minutes ago, it had been too nice of a day to be inside—but that was Texas weather for you.

Just as he putting his tools away, the bottom really fell

out—a sudden deluge of rain that he was damn glad he'd escaped. It was so loud he almost missed his ringing cell phone on the workbench, but at the last minute he noticed the lit-up display. Unfamiliar number. Ordinarily he didn't answer those, but it was local, so he relented. Could be a client with a new number, and he never wanted to miss out on work at the tattoo shop.

"Yeap," he drawled, his usual greeting that was lost somewhere between "yeah" and "yep."

"Hey dude. Long time no see."

Ghost's spine shot ramrod straight. What. The. Hell. "I don't see you now, motherfucker."

"And you haven't changed any." Mark laughed, asshole that he was. Ever since Ghost had quit his position as lead guitarist of In the Slaughter, the band Mark fronted, there had been absolutely no reason to talk to the slimy little bastard. He'd deleted all evidence of him from his phone, and his life, and had been happier for it. Mark's little brother had filled Ghost's shoes in the band, which was exactly what Mark had always wanted. Everyone's problems solved. So there.

"Have you?"

"Nah."

"Well. *That's* a problem."

"What's that noise? Is it raining?"

"What am I, the fucking weatherman? Look out your window." He slammed a cabinet shut and glanced around. Nothing was left out that Macy might ride his ass over later. His wife was a damn neat freak, even though he'd clearly specified the garage was his domain. That didn't seem to matter to her, though. "And is there some reason you're on my phone right now?"

"I can't call up an old friend?"

"You never called when we *were* friends, unless you wanted something."

Oh. Yeah, that should have occurred to him right from the start. But the only thing more interesting than fucking with Mark was finding out what Mark could possibly want.

"Okay, so you caught me. But I've got a proposition for you. Just hear me out, all right?"

"Before you even waste your breath, you know I'm walking the straight and narrow now, right? So carefully consider just how fast I'm going to tell you to fuck off before you even ask whatever it is you're going to ask."

"I heard you got married. My invitation must've gotten lost in the mail."

"Yeah, your invitation that I never sent must've gotten lost in the mail. That's it."

"Look, short and sweet," Mark began, obviously getting tired of the verbal sparring he never won, "we wanted to ask if you'd like to come back for a gig with us."

Ghost nearly laughed, wondering how many times the other guys had counseled Mark to ask as nicely as possible. Indeed, it wasn't like him. And in the split second before Ghost's phone had rung, if someone had asked him his thoughts about rejoining In the Slaughter for *any* length of time, he probably would have punched them in the face for their insolence.

But with a real offer on the table...

"I don't know, man." Macy's SUV pulled into their driveway, headlights on, windshield wipers beating furiously against the gray curtain of rain. "Hang on a second." She crept past the GTO and eased into the garage. Ghost didn't necessarily want her to hear the conversation he was having right now, so he put the phone down and helped her carry her bags into the house before hurrying back out and snatching it up again. "All right. You've got my attention. Tell me more."

"Drew broke his hand in an ATV accident. He's out for a while, but we have a show in Austin in three weeks. I know it's been a while for you. Would that be enough time to practice? It would all be familiar stuff."

"How's Gus been doing?" he asked, referring to the other guitarist and pretty much the only guy in the band Ghost gave much of a shit about.

"Well, you know. He's Gus."

Yeah, that was about what he'd expected. While he'd been in the band, he'd adopted a big-brother approach with Gus, but in the end he'd had to wash his hands of the whole thing. Too many co-dependent woman problems, too much substance abuse. You couldn't help a guy who didn't want to help himself.

Besides all of that…Ghost had bad fucking memories of the last Austin gig he'd been a part of. Between Mark and Raina scheming behind his back, and Raina damn near tricking him into fucking her when he was almost passed out, he'd nearly lost Macy. He'd watched the best thing that had ever happened to him walk away, in large part thanks to the guy on the phone who never listened to a fucking word Ghost ever said. Did he really want to get involved with that old crowd again?

"Is it at Crossbones?"

"Yeah. The usual."

"You're gonna have to let me sleep on it, man. But I gotta tell you, it's probably gonna be a no."

For the first time, a hint of desperation began to creep into Mark's voice. "If there's anything I can do, any promises I can make, anything—say the word. I'm sorry for all the shit that went down between us. It was a bad deal. I know that. And…it goes without saying that Raina will *not* be there."

No, it really didn't. Macy might have sent her running once, but his ex-girlfriend showed up wherever she damn well pleased, and if she caught wind of In the Slaughter playing in Austin with Ghost on the axe, she would be there. Oh, would she ever fucking be there. Not that she was even a blip on his radar of shit that mattered, he just preferred not to be the target of any flying beer bottles from the audience.

"Pardon me for saying that coming at me with all this shit now rings a little hollow, you know?"

"I know it must seem that way. But we need you, man. And if it's a chance to repair some shit and have a great time, it's all for the good, right?"

Sure. What could go wrong. He was being completely sarcastic, even in his head. "I'll call you back in a day or so." Jesus, did he even dare bring this up to Macy? He would have to, of course, but he fully expected that would be the final nail in the coffin of the whole idea. Macy didn't have fond memories of that night, either.

Yeah, he thought as he hung up. Macy would shoot this down. But damn, the *thrill*. Even now, he felt it awakening in his veins. No matter how much time had passed, he remembered how it felt to be up there playing on a stage. In the Slaughter had only been small-time, mostly a cover band, but he'd loved it until all the bullshit drama began to erode the friendship he'd had with his former bandmates. All of it had come to a head, and he'd bailed on the band when he and Macy were getting together, but what would one gig hurt?

Just one. Maybe she would understand.

• • •

Macy Warren glanced down at the little plastic stick on the counter, then tore her gaze away and fixed it resolutely on her reflection. Two minutes, the instructions had said. So she would give it two minutes before she looked, before she *really really* looked. She set the timer on her phone.

Had that briefest of peeks showed her the *tiniest* hint of a plus sign forming, though? Could it be?

Bouncing on her toes, she snatched her gaze higher, to the ceiling of their master bathroom. *Come on, come on.* She hadn't told Seth about her suspicions. She didn't even know if she should be *having* suspicions yet. Two days late, hell, that was pretty much the norm for her. It had been a few months since they'd thrown caution to the wind and foregone all forms of birth control, and though they weren't necessarily trying to conceive...they damn sure engaged in the act enough to make something happen.

And oh, how she wanted something to happen.

Hands laced together in front of her mouth, she turned from the vanity and paced a circle, the plush bathroom rug under her bare feet pushing between her toes. What would Seth say if it had happened? Holy shit. She was going to explode. She had to look.

No! Don't look yet.

Macy glanced at her phone. It had been one minute and forty-two seconds since she started the timer. God, she was going to die.

Just look! The result will be showing by now!

Wouldn't it? Damn, she'd never taken one of these things before.

Oh, to hell with it.

She whirled around, snatched up the stick, and looked.

Negative.

Shoulders drooping, she put it back down on the counter and thought about giving it a couple more minutes, but there was no reason to prolong the agony. The control line was evident, so she had her results. Locking gazes with her reflection again, she thought her eyes looked a little sadder.

Well...there were two tests in the box, and maybe she would take the other in the morning. That was the recommendation, anyway—take it in the morning. Maybe it was too early to detect. Or maybe she would accept defeat and save the other test until next month.

Sighing, she cleaned up and stuffed the evidence deep in the trash, wondering if she should talk to Seth about it. She hadn't actually let on to him how badly she'd wanted that test to be positive just now. The test he didn't even know she'd taken. The sole reason she'd run to the store a half-hour ago, actually, was to pick one up, though she'd given him an excuse about needing coffee creamer.

Oh well, it would happen soon. Right? Maybe next month. Or even the one after. Her mother kept telling her to enjoy their alone time while they had it, and it was true they had only been married for six months. Still, so much excitement fluttered in Macy's belly when she even thought about becoming pregnant. Getting to occasionally babysit her best friend Candace's little boy wasn't helping matters— Lyric was so sweet and adorable. Every time Candace and Brian even mentioned tentative date plans, Macy was quick to offer her services.

Not to mention that watching her bald, inked, pierced, badass husband playing with a one-year old made her want to jump his bones on the spot. Of course, she couldn't, with the kid being present and all. That might indeed be a problem once they had their own—no spontaneous sex in the kitchen. Or the laundry room. Or, hell, the front entryway.

Well, back to reality. She left the bathroom and went in search of him, remembering now that he'd been on the phone when she'd first pulled in. Abuzz with excitement over taking her very first pregnancy test ever, she hadn't even stopped to wonder who he was talking to and why he'd put them on hold to help her. She located him in the kitchen now, shirtless and throwing together a sandwich.

"Did you get the car fixed before it started raining?" she asked, walking over and standing on her tiptoes to kiss him, though he tried to duck her, the silly boy.

"Don't get too close. I probably need a shower." Like she cared. He smelled like oil and the faintest hint of the sweat that sheened his heavily inked skin, and she practically felt her ovaries growl. Oh God, yes, she wanted this man's baby. "But yeah, I hope so. Else it's gonna know *hot* when I set the fuckin' thing on fire."

"You are so not going to do that." She stole a slice of turkey breast off his sandwich and popped it into her mouth. He chuckled and replaced it with another one. "I have faith in you."

"I'm glad someone does." He slapped bread on top of his sandwich and took a bite while she thought about the struggle she'd endured only moments ago. It wasn't fair to leave him out of that. But if his disappointment turned out to be as acute as hers, then yeah, she wanted to spare him from it. She simply didn't know.

"Are you okay?" he asked suddenly, and she jerked her eyes up to find his dark, assessing ones steady on her face.

"Yeah," she said brightly. "Why wouldn't I be?"

"You want me to sell her, don't you?"

Startled, she frowned at him and shook her head. "Babe, that's completely up to you."

"But I'm asking you."

"You love that car."

"I do. And I love you."

"Well…" Macy struggled for words for a minute. The conversation had come up a handful of times before with no real resolution, and she found her feelings were mixed. On one hand, financially, it would be a burden off them. On the other… "That car *is* you." He chuckled and regarded her thoughtfully for a moment. "I just mean that you would be devastated if you got rid of her."

"Yeah," he grunted. "I would be. But your dad's friend offered a pretty decent chunk of change to take her off my hands. I've been thinking about it."

She wasn't quite sure how to put into words what she was feeling about that. Hell, maybe she was being too sentimental. But that car was such an integral part of *them* as a couple that she couldn't imagine letting it go, either. They'd talked about so much, laughed about so much in the front seat... not to mention all the naughty things that had happened in the backseat. Their first time together. Their *second* time together. She would never, could never forget those nights.

"That car is *us*," she said at last. Broken, beaten parts that had been lovingly restored. Shiny, powerful, made new again.

Sometimes, Seth's usual sardonic expression melted especially for her. She always loved those moments, when she could plainly see the adoration he had for her burning away everything else. "Baby, we're us. I don't need a car to remind me of that."

"I know," she said softly, butterflies fluttering up from her belly at the way he looked at her. "I don't either. I'm being silly, I guess. It's just sad to think about."

"Then we don't have to think about it right now."

She smiled and turned to go to the Keurig, putting an extra sway in her hips as she went, feeling his stare on her as she prepared her afternoon caffeine jolt. If she knew him— and she did—she wouldn't get around to drinking it.

• • •

It was a little game they played, where she liked to go on about her business as if he wasn't getting hard in his jeans just looking at her. They each liked to see how long the other could hold out before they ended up fucking on the spot. But he wasn't in the mood to play it, especially when she so casually began asking him about, of all things, dinner plans.

"We could do Italian, we haven't done that in a while. Or we could grill some burgers. Ooh! How about—" She turned and looked up at him with those bright hazel eyes alight, and it was his undoing. The breath rushed out of her as he caught her face in his hands and kissed her.

This, this was his favorite part of domesticity: her gorgeous body within reach at all times. The reassurance of her slender arms around him, the solidity, because sometimes he couldn't believe she was real and she wanted him.

But God, how she did. She grasped the back of his head, kissing him back as fiercely as he kissed her, each of them trying to assert their dominance, her tongue dancing into his mouth.

Letting the tips of his fingers slide around the backs of her thighs, he teased just under the hem of her shorts, eliciting a shivery groan from her. Her mouth fell open in bliss, and he took the opportunity to nibble her bottom lip, suck it gently, show her just what he would happily do to her nipples and her clit once he got her clothes off. She clung desperately, her nails biting his flesh.

On second thought, maybe he would leave her clothes on. God, he loved fucking her with her clothes on. He loved when she made it hard for him...in more ways than one.

"I love you," she murmured against his lips.

"Love you, too." Ever since the first time she'd dragged those words from his mouth, from his heart, he couldn't stop telling her.

"But you're trying to change the subject with sex."

"Yeah?" he growled, taking another taste of her. "How am I doing?"

"Hmm. Food debate, or sex...however shall I choose?"

"I'll choose for you." Each word was punctuated with a heavenly mouthful of her. Her hair slid like silk around his fingers as he stroked up her back. She still trembled for him after all this time, and he still burned for her. He always would. This woman held all the power in the world to destroy him, and like an idiot he'd willingly given it to her—but even if someday she used it, he'd have no regrets.

Her legs wrapped easily around his waist as he lifted her. They were old pros with each other's bodies by now, yet nothing was old. Every breath, every quiver, every touch… it all felt brand new and all the more devastating for their shared prowess. Equally as hot and fierce or loving and tender whether they were in their bed or the shower or he had her bent over the kitchen island.

Macy's hands busily collected the feel of him, restlessly roaming over his bare shoulders, back, and arms, as if she couldn't get enough. Even through their clothes, the heat of her pressed against his erection, rubbing deliciously, inciting him to madness. The only question was how he wanted to make her his today.

He had an idea.

"What are you doing?" she asked as he headed back toward the utility room…and the door leading to the garage.

"You'll see."

She did soon enough. Shrieking as he carried her out through the open garage door and the pouring rain hit their steaming skin like needlepoints, she clung harder, burying her face in his neck as he laughed. They had neighbors on all sides, but oh well, if they were nosy enough to watch them through their windows then they deserved whatever show they got. That had always been his philosophy, anyway.

"Are you kidding me?" she cried as he carried her to the GTO parked in the driveway. He had to release one of her delectable ass cheeks to open the passenger door, but managed to hang on to her. "It's chilly out here!"

"I'll warm you up."

"It's broad daylight!"

"It's pouring rain. Get in."

God, he loved it when the words that came from her lips were unsure, but the fire in her eyes said only *Do it, do it. Oh God, do it now.*

He'd seen the memories in her eyes earlier. Yeah, their inception had been here. This was where it all began: in his cramped backseat, struggling for the space to move together, so desperate for each other the discomfort hadn't mattered because the pleasure eclipsed it. And while they hadn't rocked the shocks back here since Valentine's Day a couple of years back, he bet nothing had changed.

Her breath hissed in as her bare legs touched the chilly upholstery. He closed the door behind him. Macy's gaze devoured the movement of his hands as he wrenched his jeans open, her chest heaving. Then those hot hazel eyes flickered up to his, and he was lost. There was only time for him to yank the soft panels of fabric between her legs aside with one fist and give her slit a teasing, readying stroke with the head of his cock, knowing he could hurt her by shoving past her initial resistance before she was ready.

But fuck, she was ready as always, wet and slick. She took him halfway with her head thrown back, her damp hair clutched in his other fist, her thighs shaking hard around his hips, before he pulled back and sank home with a groan.

Home. It wasn't just an expression. It was where he belonged, it was the place he'd spent his entire fucking life trying to find. He had it now. With her, he had it at last.

"Seth," she whimpered helplessly against his neck. Her use of his real name only fired him up more. At first, she'd only called him by his given name; now she rarely did. In public, around their friends, he was Ghost—it was only here, when it was the two of them in their little cocoon against the world, that she called him Seth, and he lived for hearing the syllable roll in sultry seduction off her tongue.

"So beautiful," he told her, watching a flush climb high in her cheeks. Drops of rain still clung to her skin and hair. Eyes dusky, locked on his and heavy-lidded with ecstasy, lips swollen and parted with the sharp breaths he pushed from her with every thrust. She enveloped him with heat and sweetness and trust and all kinds of shit he'd never thought to have. When it all became too much and he began to drop his head, her strong hands caught him and held him up. Made him stare into her eyes. Made him see the promise of forever there. He couldn't deny that it scared the hell out of him, but he stared all the same.

Knowing her cues, he could draw this out, make her cry out and beg and even curse him with the merest variation of movement. Oh, it was sweet, playing her body like his own instrument. Filing away any new discoveries for later use, pulling out old ones she might not have thought of in a while. A delectable game where they both won...though she usually reached the finish line long before he let himself.

Her first orgasm rocked her before he'd worked up a sweat. He talked her through, dropping kisses along her jaw and biting at that exquisitely quivering bottom lip while her contractions coaxed him deeper and pulled at his sanity. So wet, *fuck*, so tight. She clutched at him anywhere she could find a grip, and the heels of her running shoes dug into his ass.

"I hate you," she giggled once she could find her voice.

"Oh yeah?" Still hard, still nowhere near his breaking point, he gave her a teasing drag of his cock. She was soaked. "Let's see if I can make you hate me again."

Challenge flared deep in her eyes. Usually, once she came that hard, she was done. "You couldn't."

"Daring me will only make me try harder." He tugged at the zipper of her hoodie, skimming his fingers underneath to tease at her bare breasts. Macy's eyes closed dreamily.

Spreading the jacket aside, he bared one nipple to his sight, dipped his head to flick his tongue across the tight peak. Deep inside, her pussy clutched at him anew. "Oh, I think I could."

Rain pattered against the windows, which were already fogged up. Macy's hand rested atop his shaved head, stroking as he shifted his attentions to her other nipple. He licked and sucked and nibbled until she was ready again, growing restless beneath him, arching into his mouth, rocking her hips to take him deeper even though he denied her any real movement yet.

"Okay," she finally said on a soft chuckle, "I give in. You totally could."

"Does that mean you don't want me to?"

"You're going to be the death of me, you know that?"

"Nah. You're young and healthy, baby. You haven't killed *me* yet, so I think we're both gonna hang in for a while."

Laughing, she hugged him close. Putting his cheek to hers, he moved inside her, gentle, leisurely movements. Outside, the rain slowed, its furor spent while Ghost's gradually built. Still, he held back, even while his pulse thundered in his ears and he was so hard it hurt, instincts screaming to fuck her hard until he exploded. He lifted his head and gazed at her, finding her in the same sensuous distress.

"Are you okay?" he asked, meaning it in so much more than a physical sense. He only wanted to know she felt safe, loved, happy.

"I am," she whispered, and he believed she'd understood the depth of the question. He hoped. There was nothing left to do but give her everything. Kissing her deeply, Ghost shuddered through his own release, pulling her with him.

In the quiet moments after, while the only sound was their breathing and the last drops of rain on the roof, she said, "Seth?"

"Hmm?"

"I want a baby."

He'd already known, of course—she'd wanted to go off birth control, after all. But hearing it put so plainly, hearing the ache in her voice, undid something in him. He lifted his head and smoothed the hair back from her forehead. Her eyes were uncertain as they searched his, as if she'd been unsure of what he might say. A grin broke across his face. "Yeah?"

Macy nodded, her breath hitching. "I do. How do you feel about it?"

He only knew he wanted to make her happy—and she'd told him from the start that kids would be a part of that deal. Macy wanted to be a mom, she always had, and she deserved to be.

"I see the look in your eyes when Brian and Candace are around with Lyric," he said. "You light up."

"They're so happy."

True. But they'd gone through hell, too. Ghost and Macy had babysat for them while Brian was in the hospital recovering from an assault last year. Macy had loved every minute of the baby time; even jumping up for feedings and diaper changes at two in the morning hadn't fazed her. And Ghost had to admit, holding and feeding little Lyric had stirred a few fatherly feels in him, too. Poor little man almost had to grow up without a dad when Brian got attacked, and Ghost knew how that felt from having lost his own parents before he could form adequate memories of them.

It wasn't something he wanted to see any kid go through. Ever. He remembered looking down into that baby's innocent eyes and vowing to fill that role for him as best he could if that was the hand they got dealt. Thank God it hadn't been. Brian had recovered, good as new.

At the core of it all, though, was one almost paralyzing fear, the same one that had gripped him when his ex, Raina, had come to him with news that she was pregnant. She'd lost their baby, but memories of the funk he'd walked around in for weeks were still vivid. "What if I'm a shitty dad?"

"Please. You'll be an amazing dad. Besides, you'll have me. We'll be a team."

That was so undeniably true. Parenting a kid with Macy would be at the opposite end of the spectrum from parenting with someone like Raina. An idea filled with hope versus one filled with dread.

Still beneath him, Macy licked her lips and glanced up at him uncertainly. "I kind of thought I might already be pregnant, but I took a test and it was negative." She rushed that last bit out, as if she was afraid he might have an immediate breakdown at the news. It was only the disappointment in her eyes that broke something in him.

"Aw, babe," he said gently, touching her cheek. "You should've told me."

"I know. I was so excited and nervous, I thought I would see if there was anything to freak out over before I freaked you out." She chuckled sadly.

"That's what's been bothering you, then?"

"Yeah, a little."

No, it was a lot. He knew her better than that. "Well, maybe..." With a sheepish smirk, he glanced down to where their bodies were still joined and raised his eyebrows meaningfully. Maybe they'd just accomplished the deed a few minutes ago.

Macy grinned but shook her head. "Nah, I doubt it. It's not the right time for me."

Gently pulling from her body, he opened his mouth to reply that she should tell him when it was, and they would go at it like rabbits. But his phone buzzed in the back pocket of the jeans hanging loose around his ass. With a growl of frustration, he was prepared to let it go to voicemail, but with a kiss Macy told him, "It's okay, go ahead."

Chapter Two

When Ghost pulled out his phone and saw the name on the display, he immediately shoved the device back into his pocket. "Nah, I'll get it later." And then he realized how shady that sounded.

"Who is it?" Macy asked as he straightened in the seat, allowing her to sit up and tug her clothing back into place.

It was Gus, his former bandmate, no doubt wanting to add his voice to Mark's in begging him back to the group. He couldn't not answer her, even if he wasn't quite ready to explain the situation. "It's Gus."

She turned incredulous eyes on him as she zipped her jacket and he zipped up his jeans. "The drug addict?"

Jesus, leave it to her to cut to the heart of the matter. "Yeah."

"I didn't know you talked to those guys anymore."

"I don't, usually." Except for one night several months back, when he was assisting Macy's ex in the hunt for the drugged-out asshole who'd attacked Brian, Ghost hadn't spoken to Gus since he quit In the Slaughter. But he'd needed him that night, because Gus knew all the drugged-out assholes and which rocks to overturn to find them.

"I wonder what he could want," she mused.

Sighing, Ghost turned his attention out the window. The rain was a soft, lazy patter now, the kind that made you want to slip under the sheets and doze until it was over. Despite that desire, he felt jittery, disconsolate. He bounced one knee and felt Macy's gaze on him. Finally, he turned to meet it, figuring there was no time like the present.

"I've sort of been invited back for a gig."

"Oh, Seth…" Trailing off, she let her head meet the back of the seat. "You aren't considering it, are you?"

"Funny part about it is…yeah, I am."

"I don't like it."

"I didn't think you would."

"You know that, but you're still considering it?"

"I thought you would at least hear my case before you rendered a verdict."

She shrugged, suddenly seeming very interested in picking at a fingernail. "Okay. Begin."

"Now? You haven't given me time to build my argument."

Giggling, she reached over and put her hand on his, her slender fingers giving his a squeeze. "When would it be?"

"He said three weeks from now."

"Where?"

"Austin. Same place you came to that night…you know." He scratched his head with his free hand, cringing inwardly.

"Oh, Jesus! This keeps getting worse. Would *she* be around? She moved back there, didn't she?"

"Honestly, babe, I don't know where Raina is. Out of my life, that's for damn sure. But whether or not she's still in Austin, or wherever the fuck she went…I have no clue. Don't wanna know, don't care."

"I know that, but I can damn well guarantee you she

cares where *you* are."

"I think you scared her off me."

"And I think seeing you again would set it all back in motion. It's too risky."

Maybe she was right. Still, it grated to think of missing an opportunity he wanted because of an unrelenting ex he didn't give a shit about. "It's done. She would know right away she doesn't have a shot. I really don't think there's anything to worry about, Mace."

"You know what she did...what she almost made you do." He wasn't likely to forget. He'd been drunk off his ass, missing Macy so bad it was a physical pain in his chest, and Raina had tried to seduce him in a back office of the venue when he was only semiconscious. Macy had walked in at a very inopportune moment. Ghost still wanted to unzip his own skin and shed it whenever he thought of her seeing him like that.

They sat silently for a moment, lost in ugly memories. Finally Macy said, "It would drive me crazy sitting here worried about you."

"Hey, wait a minute," he cut in. "You would come, too."

She looked at him in surprise. "I would, huh?"

"Hell yes, you would. You never got to see me perform before I quit."

"Don't do this on my account." She nudged his arm. "You serenade me all the time; that's all I need."

"Come on, babe," he goaded, "don't you want to see me in action?"

Grasping his chin, she made him look her in the eyes. "That action I just got? That's the only action I care about."

"I think you'd get a kick out of it. We could invite Brian and Candace, see if they could get a sitter for the night. It would be fun. Plus," he added, reaching up to take her hand and pull it to his lips. "There's that little matter we need to work on. Come with me and we'll work on it day and night. All weekend. On the trip there, on the trip back, and every spare minute in between."

Her eyes widened. "Are you seriously bribing me with baby-making sex?"

"Bribing you? No. I'm *negotiating*."

Suddenly, though, she pulled away, severing all contact with him, and simply faced forward with a frown. "I'm just really confused as to why you seem to want to do this so much. I thought you'd left all that behind. *Happily.* So please understand why I'm taken aback."

"I do understand. I was taken aback, too. My first impulse was to tell Mark to stick it when he called and asked. But...I couldn't say the words. I did love it, you know. I loved playing, I loved the music. It's the people I had a problem with, but I figure, dealing with them for a few weeks is a small price to pay to do something I love again."

"Will one gig lead to two, and then three, and then suddenly you're back in for good?"

He shook his head. "Nah."

"Is it possible?"

"I guess any fucking thing is possible. But it isn't likely, and I'm not counting on it."

"I don't like it," she said firmly, repeating her earlier verdict. "I saw some of the things that were going on in that place when I was there."

"Just because you saw things going on doesn't mean I'll be doing them. I'm not gonna fuck up what we have, baby. I was on the road to Fuckupsville for the entirety of my life. Now I'm off, and I like the scenery over here much better."

"Then...why do you need to go back there? Even for a night?"

He really didn't have an answer for that. So he kept his mouth shut, because his mouth had the ability to get him into trouble he wasn't looking for.

"Is this because you're feeling trapped?" she asked.

"What?"

"We've barely been married six months, and you want to go back to things you left when we first started seeing each other. It's freaking me out, I'm sorry. Like maybe you think you made a mistake or—"

"I promise you, that is *not* it. I have no motives other than wanting to play. I'm pretty sure they have none other than needing a replacement on short notice. That's it. Okay?"

Now it was her turn to fall silent for a while, long enough for the gentle pattering of the rain to become occasional plops. Finally, about to leap out of his skin with frustration, he said, "So...not okay?"

She still didn't look at him. Her voice was sad, and that killed him. "It's up to you. But I'm not going."

"If it upsets you that much, forget it. I won't do it."

"No, no. You go do it. I'm not going to tell you that you can't. I don't think I can be there to see it, though. I'm sorry."

"I want you there, baby."

The way she looked at him then, so direct, so final, dashed his hopes to pieces. What was the point, really, if she wouldn't be there to see it? He wanted her by his side in all things. It was why he'd married her. But she shook her head. "I can't."

• • •

Seth usually wasn't one to sulk or give her the silent treatment when she pissed him off. He liked to fight it out, yell if they needed to—and end the argument with hot make-up sex that left them both too exhausted to think about it anymore.

But he was troublingly quiet for the rest of the day, even later while he was grilling burgers and they each drank a beer on the back patio, listening to the kids next door play in their backyard swimming pool. They couldn't see the kids for the privacy fence, but it sounded like they were having a blast. Macy twirled and untwirled a piece of hair around her finger and focused on their splashing and laughter, imagining a day when she might hear it from her own backyard.

"We need to move," he grumbled as he sat in the chair next to her, then took a hefty pull on his beer bottle.

She turned a frown on him. "What? Why?"

"Neighbors on all fucking sides." He flipped the aviator sunglass from the top of his head to his eyes, shielding them from her. And it wasn't even bright out, but heavily overcast from the recent rain, with twilight creeping in.

"They're just kids having fun," she protested.

"It's not even about the kids, really, more about their asshole parents."

"But…" Macy was momentarily at a loss. "You grew up here."

"So?"

"It's the first time you've ever mentioned moving, that's all. I had no idea you were even considering it." First the car, then the band, now this… What other things did he have going on in his head that she had no clue about?

"If I had my way," he said, "we'd live in the middle of nowhere, with at least a mile between us and the next house, where I wouldn't have someone up my ass when I'm mowing the fucking lawn or working on the car or whatever else. Somewhere I could play my music or rev my engine as loud as I wanted without getting the side-eye from the jerkoff across the street."

"Why are you so hostile right now?"

He looked at her, but with those damn sunglasses in place, she couldn't tell a thing about his expression. "Am I hostile?"

"You're mad at me, aren't you?"

"No."

"You're mad in general."

He scoffed and took another drink of beer. Macy seized the opportunity to do the same; she felt she needed it if she was really about to say the words crowding for release behind her lips.

"If you're going to act like a baby for the rest of the night because we had one disagreement—"

Grumbling something unintelligible, he jumped up with the spatula in hand to flip the burgers.

"Don't walk away from me."

He didn't reply. She was left staring at his back while smoke rose around him and a delicious sizzle sounded from the grill. He did make some damn good burgers. Her stomach grumbled at the scent.

"Seth..."

"Macy."

"I'm sorry. I'm just not comfortable with the whole band thing. You know that's...not my scene."

He turned around then, pushing his sunglasses to the top of his head and hitting her with the full force of his dark eyes' devastating intensity. "As if your rodeo shit is my scene."

Macy opened her mouth, then promptly clamped it shut. He'd been waiting for that, hadn't he? She wondered, briefly, if it was okay to momentarily hate your husband. Just for a second. He arched one eyebrow, awaiting her reply.

There was none she could make. None whatsoever.

But...but...but...rejoining your band might put you in the vicinity of your ex.

Her "rodeo shit" put her in the vicinity of hers. Jared had never been as possessive as Raina in his endeavors to get Macy back, but yeah, once upon a time he'd damn near broken her and Seth up. He was happily engaged to Seth's coworker Starla now, though, something that greatly relieved

Macy. Jared was a good guy and deserved someone who loved him the same way he was capable of loving. Macy had never been that person, but Starla was.

Still, whenever they all happened to show up at the same place, it was a bit awkward, even though Seth had admitted he'd come around and actually liked Jared. A little, he'd quickly amended, but Macy wasn't fooled. That "little" was miraculous in itself.

When she continued to look at him, he went on. "I'm always there for you with that stuff. Always. No, I don't like it. But I don't let on to you how much I don't like it. I go anyway, and cheer you on, and deal with everyone looking at me like 'What the fuck is *that* guy doing here,' and I've never complained, not one time, at least not until now. Have I?"

"No," she admitted. "Not that I can recall."

"Thing is, I wouldn't have complained now. I would have kept going for you, whenever and wherever you want, because that's your thing and I love you and support you in it."

"You don't have to go."

"I do it for you."

"But…"

"Macy." He leveled her with a long look. She met it for as long as her resolve would allow, then finally threw her hands in the air.

"All right! Fine. You do it, and I'll go with you. But don't mind me if I sulk for the rest of the night like you have all day."

He grinned. "Deal."

She stuck her bottom lip out at him in a grossly exaggerated pout.

"You'd better put that back in before I bite it." Ignoring the comment, she sat back and crossed one leg over the other. He went on. "Look, I'll make a deal with you. I'll go practice with them a couple of times. Could be we'll sound like shit, or someone will piss me off, or it just won't work out. At that point, I'm gone. So whether or not you should go will be a moot point."

That sounded reasonable, she supposed, only she knew better than to get her hopes up. "All right. Two practices," she relented. "If you get even a *hint* of a bad feeling about it all, you have to back out, Seth. Promise me."

He shrugged, then grinned like the cat who'd had the cream. "I promise, baby. Easy."

Sighing, Macy decided to let it go for now. There was only one full day a week she got to spend with him, and she'd be damned if she would spend the rest of it letting this eat at her.

Chapter Three

He strolled into Dermamania on Tuesday ten minutes late, head down, hoping no one noticed. Wishful thinking. Brian Ross, his best friend and boss, missed nothing. As he slipped by the office heading for the front, Brian called out to him.

"Where the fuck you been?"

Ghost rubbed at the back of his head sheepishly. "Oh, my brother, you don't want to know."

Brian cocked a dark eyebrow at him, but took him at his word and went back to whatever art masterpiece he was sketching out. Ghost hung out in the door and watched him for a minute, considering what his best bud since freshman year of high school would have to say about him rejoining In the Slaughter. There would probably be some good counsel there, even if it wasn't something he wanted to hear.

"So…how are things?" Ghost asked at last.

Brian looked up at him, really seeing him for the first time. "What's the matter with you?" His friend knew him well.

"Mark invited me back to play a gig with them. I want to

do it."

"What the hell for?"

Yeah, that was pretty much the reaction he'd counted on. "I don't know, man. Relive my days of glory?"

"*Those* were your days of glory?"

Good point. "At times, they were pretty fuckin' stellar."

"It's all changed up now. Those days are dead and gone. Those guys, though…they're stuck back there. Do you think they've changed any? I can guarantee you, they haven't. But *you* have."

Brian had been there the night the shit hit the fan backstage at Crossbones. He'd seen the whole ugly business: Macy distraught and screaming, Ghost staggering drunk, Raina gloating about something that hadn't happened. "It would only be for one gig. I thought I'd help out, I don't know."

"What does Macy think?"

"Need you ask? Especially now, when she has a baby on the brain?"

Brian's eyes widened for a second, then he burst out laughing, the bastard. "*That's* where you've been. Congratulations."

Shit, Brian didn't know. Ghost had thought for sure that Macy had discussed her desires with Candace, who told Brian everything. "It's a little premature for congrats. I didn't say she's *having* a kid. Yet."

"Don't be too premature, or you'll never get the deed done."

"Ha. Fucking. Ha."

Brian raised his eyebrows. "No comeback? Don't be so dour. I'm sure it's only a matter of time."

"I damn sure won't mind working at it."

"Dude? That's something I don't need to hear about."

Ghost chuckled, finally walking into Brian's office and

dropping into one of the chairs that faced his desk, where the employees all sat to shoot the shit or sometimes get their asses chewed out. "But this is the part where you tell me how big a step it is and scare the shit out of me."

"I'm here to tell you it's a bigger step than you can even contemplate right now. But it's a great one. I wouldn't change it for the world."

"Good to know." If there was one hang-up Ghost had about that baby thing, it was that he'd actually found a beautiful, perfect woman who *wanted* to be afflicted with his hellspawn, so there had to be something wrong with her. What kind of glitch in the Matrix had caused this shit to happen, and how long before they fixed it so that everything went to hell again? He couldn't think too hard about it. "So…I don't suppose I could count on you to be in the audience next month."

With a shrug, Brian idly picked up his cell phone when it pinged to read an incoming text. "Maybe I could be. When is it?"

"The eighteenth."

"Yeah, Candace and I could use a getaway for a night. Mom would be more than thrilled to keep Lyric." He glanced up from his phone with a grin. "All spontaneity goes out the window when you have a kid, you see. Everything becomes a plan."

"Yeah, I know. But everyone else makes it work, you guys make it work, so we'll make it work, too, I'm sure."

"Are you hoping for one last party before you resign yourself to your fate, or what? Because I thought we took care of that at your bachelor party."

Oh God, what a night that had been. While he'd been a good boy—pretty good, anyway—the Dermamania crew had whisked him away for a surprise whirlwind two-night Vegas trip, and some of the shenanigans had made him more grateful than ever that he would be waking up with the same woman for the rest of his life. The shark-infested waters of singledom held absolutely no appeal anymore. For a guy celebrating his last hurrah as a bachelor, he'd practically been the boring one.

"Can't I do one thing without everyone analyzing my fuckin' motives? You're as bad as Macy."

"Don't dick me around. Let's not forget how long I've known you. Hell, I know you better than she does."

That was probably true. Still. "I liked playing live music. I liked being onstage. I miss it. I have my one shot to do it again and I want to. It's really as simple as that."

"Why don't you just put out the word you want to join another band? We have connections."

"I don't really want to go through all that, so why don't I just do this?"

Brian shrugged and pushed up out of his chair. He twisted his black baseball cap around backward. "Do what you gotta. I should have an appointment here in a few minutes."

Ghost did, too, though he would rather stay and argue. Macy was heavy on his mind…he'd come directly here from lunch at her office, where she'd locked her door and let him bang her on her desk, their mouths crushed together to stifle each other's groans. Fuck, it had been hot; he was still half hard thinking about it. She didn't think it was her fertile time, but what the hell, might as well cover all the bases, and he damn sure couldn't get inside her fast enough when she gave him the *look*. That molten, heavy-lidded stare of hers that went straight to his dick.

He loved that woman more than anything else in the world. She was his heart. But hanging on to a little bit of himself was necessary, too, hence this need to play another show. It had been a struggle from the very beginning not to give her every last piece of his fucking soul, let her consume him completely. And she was good at that, good at getting things her way, and he didn't think she even realized when she did it. For the most part, he let her have it, but he did choose his battles carefully.

He had to admit, though, if Macy eventually put that size-seven cowgirl boot down and said "This is the way it's gonna be, jackass," he might roll over like a whipped dog. That scared him. He hoped it never came to that between them. She wanted a kid, he was cool with that. She needed to be cool with this. Maybe Brian had been more right than he knew when he suggested this was a last hurrah.

When his client appeared to be running late—it was in the air, it seemed—he took a minute to send his wife a text.

Pregnant yet?

LOL! Not that I'm aware of.

I'm just saying, that should've gotten the job done.

I think everyone knows what we were in here doing. They've all been grinning at me.

He chuckled when he read that. She managed her parents' sporting goods store, and the employees had learned not to bother her when he showed up during her lunch hour. Aside from that, Macy *wore* great sex. It brightened her up. Put color in her cheeks, a sparkle in her eyes—it was one of his favorite things about her: watching her walk around all lit up and knowing he'd flipped that particular switch.

Awesome, he told her.

Why is that awesome?

Because you're mine and everyone better fuckin know it.

Oooh. I like it when you get all alpha.

I'm always alpha, baby.

I miss you!

And his heart went straight to goo. Yeah, so he'd left her less than half an hour ago. He missed the hell out of her. In a perfect world, they wouldn't need jobs and could stay in bed working on making that baby all day, every day. *Miss you, too, babe*, he told her, then grudgingly tucked his phone away.

Their schedules were not ideal. She worked nine to six, Monday through Friday. He worked two to ten on a good day...until eleven or twelve when they were super busy, with Sunday his only consistent day off. Usually he was off Mondays, too, though he would set appointments sometimes if his clients needed it.

He hated knowing when she left in the mornings that he wouldn't see her again until late that night unless he went by her workplace before he headed to his own at two o'clock. Going to her job every day made him feel like a pest, so he made a point to only do it a couple times a week. Likewise, she would sometimes swing by Dermamania to see him on her way home from work, or bring him dinner, but if he had someone under the needle, he didn't have time to talk to her.

It sucked. While he was in the middle of stewing over the injustice of it all, Candace, Brian's wife, came in with their son on her hip. Lyric was a cute little stinker, with a mop of black hair like Brian's and some very chubby cheeks. Ghost envied his best friend at that moment. He would love it if Macy could breeze in the doors whenever she felt like it. Kid in tow, even. A strange pang hit him in the chest at the thought. He'd always thought he wanted that for her, but mostly, right then, he wanted it for him.

"What the hell are you thinking?" he heard Candace demand, but didn't look up from wiping down his counter because he never would have possibly assumed by her tone that she was talking to *him*. When laughter erupted and Brian called his name, though, he turned with an eyebrow cocked.

"Huh?"

Candace had handed Lyric over to Brian. She propped both hands on her hips and gave Ghost a death stare. "You're making Macy go to Crossbones again? After what happened there?"

He shot Brian a withering look. "News travels fast. And she *agreed,* you know."

"Agreed, or was coerced?" Candace fired back. These two were outrageously protective of each other. The older they got, the worse they were.

"We negotiated. We *compromised.* That's what marriage is all about, don't you know? Hell, y'all have been married longer than we have, and here I am giving you advice."

Candace rolled her eyes. "Well, I can't let her go there by herself."

"Who the fuck said she'll be by herself? She's going with me."

"You'll be onstage most of the time, genius."

"For thirty minutes tops. She's a grown woman. But yeah, you guys should come. I already invited your worse half." Not that he'd even told Mark for certain that he was doing this thing yet. It wasn't really a conversation to look forward to. Even though it was something Ghost wanted to do, giving that asshole his way was definitely one major con.

"I said we could use the getaway," Brian told Candace, ruffling his son's messy hair while the boy giggled around the teething ring grasped in his chubby fists. "I could do with some live music. It's been too long."

"So you're going," Ghost said. "It's decided. Stop bitching me out, because we're all gonna have a good time."

Candace didn't look convinced. "You'd better be extra nice to her in these next few weeks to make up for this," she said, glaring at him.

He grinned at her. That had never been a problem. "Don't worry. I'll be extra-*special* nice to your bestie."

• • •

Does he seem okay to you?

Macy hit send on the message to Candace and chewed her bottom lip as she awaited the response. It seemed rather ridiculous and juvenile to be reduced to asking her best friend about her own husband, but sometimes she felt like Seth shut her out. She'd had that feeling since their argument in the back of his car.

We got into it. Other than that, he's kind of quiet today, Candace replied.

Of all the adjectives in the world to describe Seth Warren, *quiet* was the least of them—or at least it should be.

You got into it? What do you mean?

I can't believe he's asking you to go back there and I told him so.

Wincing, Macy typed furiously. *Please don't, it's okay. What's he doing?*

With a client right now.

She drew a deep breath. She was a little jealous of that person. He'd given Macy her one and only tattoo, a large ivy pattern to cover the surgery scar on her back, and it had been an experience she would never forget. Though it had taken hours and hurt like hell, she'd loved letting him create his art on her skin. It had been as intimate as everything else they did together, as everything that had happened in her office an hour ago. And while she didn't know that she wanted any more work done, it was something she would treasure always.

What are you worried about? Candace asked, and hell, she didn't know. Being worried about anything seemed ridiculous.

I'm not even sure. I just have a weird feeling.

You shouldn't.

Thanks.

Stress? Anxiety? She wanted a baby so badly, and the band thing irked her, and she wasn't even sure why. Maybe because she was settling down, thinking of quiet nights at home with family, and suddenly he'd whisked her back to the same feelings she'd had when they were first dating. The uncertainty about who he was, what he wanted, and how compatible they were. Or weren't.

Raina was also a factor, certainly, but not because Macy felt threatened. Seth couldn't even stand being in the same room with the woman. It was only, if he wanted to start a family with Macy, why did he feel the need to hook up with past influences? *Bad* influences? That wasn't the life she wanted, sitting at home with the kids while her husband chased rock stardom. He'd insisted for as long as she'd known him that a career in music had never been his ambition—he enjoyed playing, and that was that. But what if that changed? Anything could change. She didn't like the opportunities this presented him. They scared her.

Did he regret giving all that up to marry her? Try as she might, it was the only conclusion she could come to: there were elements of his past that he missed. If he wanted to play live music, a guy as talented as him could find other opportunities. Why go back?

Try as she might, she couldn't focus on work; her computer screen blurred in front of her eyes, and she kept thinking about what he'd done to her just a couple of feet away from where she sat right now. The way he'd shoved her over on her desk and drove into her as if he had some hidden aggression to work out. She'd taken it all, his hands rough on her, his thrusts deep and punishing. Her fingers had gripped the desk's edge so hard her joints still ached, and every time she shifted in her chair she felt the shape of him inside her. Jesus. It had been hot, and as silent as they could make it, and her heart still turned little flips when aftershocks rocked her. She'd come twice before he had once.

He *had* sent her that cute message asking if she was

pregnant yet. She was worrying for nothing. He hadn't denied her anything. She closed her eyes in bliss to think of it.

But, as she'd told him in his car, it wasn't the right time. All her worrying was probably just a rampant case of PMS, and any day now, "Shark Week" would commence, as she called it. Well, she would be damn glad when it came and went.

Wait a minute. Glancing at her calendar, she frowned, then burst out laughing. Of course. The show was in three weeks, he'd said...right at her peak ovulation time. She hadn't quite realized just how perfect that timing would be. Well, she hoped he was ready, because he might not be capable of going onstage when she was through with him. That was one surefire way to keep Seth Warren from getting into too much trouble at the concert.

Macy grinned and went back to her computer, feeling a little better about the whole thing. When they went to Austin, he would *definitely* make good on his end of the bargain. She was going to fuck him until he could barely walk.

Chapter Four

Dermamania was sometimes Grand Central fucking Station. People liked to come by with their friends just to hang out. At any given moment, customers were browsing the flash, the T-shirts Candace had designed, shooting the shit with each other and the artists, even when they had no intention of going under the needle. It was a good, laid-back, easy atmosphere. Most nights. It also sometimes attracted drunk assholes, and more than a few times, they had to point out the sign on the wall: *If you are drunk, stoned, stupid, stinky, dirty, sunburned, sick, pregnant, rude, broke, looking for a deal or otherwise just plain loud or obnoxious...please come back when you are not.*

Of course, as Ghost so often jokingly pointed out, with few exceptions, stupid, rude, broke, loud, and obnoxious described a lot of their clients and even the people who worked there. Usually, it was all good. Until it wasn't.

Highly Suspect's "Claudeland" bounced enthusiastically from the speakers while the clock ticked ever closer to closing time. The group that sauntered in then consisted of three guys and a couple of girls, and the signs were readily apparent: flushed cheeks, loud, the invincible swagger of the inebriated. Ghost shot Brian a glance as one of the guys approached Janelle, who was just cleaning up after a session. Right away he saw that the boss man had his eye on the situation, too.

So much shit had gone down here. Candace's brother trashing the place. Brian getting stabbed and damn near dying in the parking lot. After all the hits they'd taken, they'd built something worth fighting for, and none of them were prepared to put up with any bullshit. As soon as it was obvious Janelle was refusing service and the drunk dude started to raise his voice, Brian was abandoning his work to take the lead, with Ghost right by his side.

"What's the problem?" Brian asked, that authoritative steel in his voice that only came from years of dealing with this type of prick.

"Get within six feet of him and you'll know," Janelle said.

"I don't have to." Brian shifted his gaze to the guy. "You were swaying on your feet when you walked in the door, man. Sober up, come back in a night or two, and we'll fix you up."

"Dude, fuck that, I'm fine. I only had a couple."

"A couple forties, maybe," Ghost said. He could never really be counted on to de-escalate a situation; he knew this about himself. Brian probably preferred him to hang back and keep his mouth shut. Impossible expectation when someone was being a dick to his friends. Unfortunately, Macy took that moment to walk in the door, stopping short and raising her eyebrows when she took in the unfolding conflict.

"Come on, Rich," one of the girls said. "Their work isn't all that great anyway."

Macy sent the girl a death stare, her mouth lengthening into a thin line, but she didn't say anything. Thank God, because he didn't need to be pulling his wife out of a brawl… which she would undoubtedly win.

"I wanna talk to the owner," Rich insisted, bleary eyes barely focusing on either Ghost or Brian.

"Oh, all right, hang on, I'll get him," Ghost said, then shoved Brian in the arm. "They need you, dude."

Brian shot Ghost a look as Rich gaped a little, but he continued trying to defuse the situation and get them out the door as peacefully as possible while Ghost watched Macy walk through to the back to wait on him. Actually, he watched her because he was waiting for one of the drunk douchebags to even *look* at her the wrong way, or God forbid, speak to her. Every one of his bodily systems was on high alert, waiting for go time. Lucky for the group, they were occupied with trying to drag their friend out the door, insisting there were better places to go.

For them, yeah, there was any number of scratchers out there who would be more than happy to carve some abomination into their sweaty, alcohol-secreting skin. It wasn't here, and it damn sure wasn't tonight.

"Thanks," Janelle said dully to Brian, shaking her head as the crowd finally staggered out. "Fucking asshats."

"No problem." Brian went over to turn off the Open sign and lock the door behind them. "Think that's enough for the night," he remarked, even though there were twenty minutes still on the clock.

Macy was perched on Ghost's chair, watching him a little wide-eyed as he headed toward her.

"You okay?" he asked. He hadn't expected to see her here tonight.

"Oh, yeah, fine," she said and gestured toward the door as Brian and Jan headed toward the back, still talking about the incident. "Does that happen here very often?"

"Not too often," he said, idly straightening some of his ink bottles.

"Hmm." Her hazel eyes watched his hands for a moment,

then she smiled and looked at him. "I thought I'd stop by. I got lonely and I didn't know how late you'd be."

That wasn't like her...the whole lonely thing. She was pretty damn independent, and besides that, she had a dozen people she could call or hang out with. He raised an eyebrow. "Is everything okay, babe?"

"Let's go home," she said, glancing around. "I'm fine, though."

He grabbed his keys and gave them a twirl around his finger, not buying her assurances for a minute. "You eat anything?" he asked. She was bad about skipping meals when she was stressed out for any reason. At this hour, though, they didn't have many options that didn't involve a drive-thru window.

"No."

"Damn, baby. Let's get you fed." He shrugged into his hoodie and grabbed her hand. "I'm out," he called to Brian and Janelle, then led his wife out the side door.

"I'm really not hungry," she protested.

"Then tell me what's wrong," he said, stopping by his car to open the passenger door for her. She slid inside, and he had to marvel, as always, at how fucking good she looked sitting there. Hell, how could he ever sell his car and abandon this sight? It had all started right here. This car, this parking lot. Her smooth legs around his hips. Her warmth gripping him. Her cries in his ear.

"What are you doing?" she asked, looking up at him, and he realized he'd been staring.

"Nothing." Blowing out a breath, he shut her door and jogged around to the driver's side. Once settled inside, he turned to face her. "Look. Let's cut through the shit. The part where I ask you what's wrong ten times and you say 'nothing' every time even though I can *clearly* see something is bothering you. Let's skip that, because it's useless, and get to what's eating at you. Is it the gig, still?"

She giggled. "I don't do that."

"Yes, you do."

"Well...you do, too."

"Touché. But I'm not doing it right now, you are. And you're deflecting."

"I love you."

He burst out laughing. "*Stop*. God."

"I don't know. I'm just in a funk. No, the gig isn't helping. But we'll get through it and it'll be all right." Macy waved a dismissive hand. "So feed me or whatever."

Clicking his tongue as he turned away to crank the car, he couldn't let that one pass him by. "I got somethin' to feed you, baby."

Of course, his music was so earsplittingly loud she jumped when it screamed from the speakers, and he quickly reached to turn it down. "You're gonna be deaf by the time you're forty," she scolded.

"Then I won't have to listen to your cowboy bullshit."

"You won't listen to your cow-decapitating, blood-sacrificing bullshit, either."

He laughed at that, loving how she could flip his shit back at him without batting an eye. But it wasn't until later, after they'd stuffed themselves with tacos and were lying in bed with every inch of her warm, naked body spooned against his, that she finally opened up.

"Your job is starting to make me nervous," she admitted, her thumb stroking his hand.

Ghost felt himself stiffen, and not in a good way. "Why?"

"It just seems like a lot of bad stuff happens there."

"Come on, Mace. That's ridiculous."

"How? First it got vandalized—"

"We had your very best friend's brother to thank for that. Let's not forget."

"I know. But then Brian almost got killed there. Completely separate incident. If something had happened to you—"

"That asshole would have struck out at Brian no matter where he was. He was just an easy target, leaving work by himself late at night." Even thinking about Max and what he'd tried to do made renewed fury seep through his veins. Very little in Ghost's life had been more satisfying than helping to bring that fuckstain down.

"I walked in tonight and I was afraid you guys were about to go off," she admitted. "It was scary."

"Maybe we're a little on edge after what we've been through, yeah. There are people we dread seeing walk in the door. I won't lie. But ninety-eight percent of our clientele is cool."

"It's not getting worse or anything?"

"No. Not at all. Shit like that happens. I'm sorry you happened to see it." He trailed his hand up her smooth arm, over the roundness of her shoulder to trace her delicate collarbone, and then moved her long dark hair from around her neck.

Just as she shivered, as he'd known she would, he dropped a kiss on the side of her neck. He began to stiffen in the *good* way, and she chuckled when she felt it. The throaty sound only exacerbated the situation. "Again?" she asked.

"The fuck you mean, *again*? Like it's weird or something. Have you even met me? Do I need to reintroduce you?" When he nibbled where he'd kissed a moment ago, she laughed, her body squirming back against him. And when he let his roaming hand slip between her legs, he found her wet. Hot. Her breath quickened as he pushed in. "You drive me fucking crazy, you know that?" he rasped in her ear.

"You show me…fairly often," she said, the words broken with a sigh as he dragged his fingers out and in again. Then she turned her head, her mouth seeking his in the darkness, and there wasn't any more need for words.

· · ·

"All right, man. I'm in." Ghost made the announcement over the phone to Mark the next day, but quickly cut off the singer's outburst of joy. "Hold up. I swear to Christ, dude, if I get just one bad vibe about this thing, I'm out. You got me? Because I'm fucking serious. I don't care if we're plugging in, about to go onstage. One cross word, hell, one cross *look*, and I'm out of there before you can even call me a fucking asshole."

"Understood."

"You sure about that?"

"I hear you. I know there've been some bad feelings in the past, I get it. We're not about that anymore."

"Good. When do we practice? It'll have to be late. We're busier than we've ever been at work so I'm not about to abandon Brian."

"We can work with it. Whenever you can make it is when we'll do it."

Yeah, but Macy wouldn't like it, and Ghost didn't like anything that cut into Macy time. But like she said, it was only for a few weeks.

He left the bedroom five minutes later, after setting a tentative practice schedule and hanging up as soon as he could get away. Macy waited in the kitchen, fingers wrapped around a mug of coffee, eyebrows raised expectantly. "Looks like we're all set," he told her.

To his surprise, she only gave a strange little smile and sipped from her cup before nodding. "Okay."

"We'll practice on Sundays and Mondays when I'm off. Maybe after I get off some nights if we need to. I think we ought to still be pretty tight, though. It'll be mostly familiar stuff."

"That's good," she said nonchalantly.

Her demeanor gave him pause, and he studied her for a few seconds. She was being way more accommodating than he'd anticipated. Which could very well spell disaster. "Annnd...you're okay?"

"I'm okay."

"No, you aren't."

Something about that made her laugh, the laugh that did him in more often than not, pretty hazel eyes sparkling, her perfect lips the perfect frame for her perfect teeth, and she was just too fucking *perfect*. "I'm fine. It's fine. Do what you have to do, baby."

"You're up to something."

And that made her laugh harder. Jesus Christ, for all her perfection, the woman was evil. But just as quickly as her laugh had come, she suppressed it, though the remnants still brightened her eyes. She twirled a long swath of dark hair around her finger. "I'm not up to anything. Go do your practices whenever you need to. We'll have fun on our trip. Lots of fun. I'm sorry I was such a bitch about everything."

"Babe, you're never a bitch."

"Well, thanks?" She downed the rest of her coffee, rinsed the cup, and set it in the sink. "It'll be fun to watch you onstage. I can admit it."

That's what he'd wanted to hear all along. He grinned, walking up behind her to wrap his arms around her waist, inhaling the vanilla scent of her freshly washed hair. "I'll put on a good show for you, babe."

Macy turned within the circle of his arms and slid her hands around the back of his neck, standing on tiptoe to kiss him. She swept her thumb across his lips. "Oh, I know you will."

Chapter Five

The practices went well, better than he could have ever expected. For one, Mark wasn't an asshole. Secondly, Gus actually showed up and worked and seemed to be on the wagon. Ghost liked to think it was because he was back, and the two of them had always been powerhouses who fed well off each other. Maybe, maybe not. Whatever the reason, it was good, and they sounded stellar, like old times. If it had always been that way, it's possible he would never have left in the first place.

But then so many things might be different.

As the date crept nearer, Candace and Brian decided to join them, but they wanted to ride separately...apparently they needed some rare alone time, too. Brian's parents agreed to keep Lyric for the night.

"I'm so glad they could come," Macy said when they were finally on the road for the three-hour drive to Crossbones in Austin...a drive that mostly consisted of a two-lane highway and sucked because there were always tractors and chicken trucks and shit like that to get stuck behind. Had to love

Texas.

"Me, too. You'll definitely have more fun with them around."

"I think both their sets of parents practically fight over who gets Lyric when they go away for a night."

"Yeah."

"If you're worried, you know, about our spontaneity going out the window when we have a baby? We'll always have my parents to lean on if we need them. They can't wait to be grandparents."

"I know that," he said simply, staring ahead through his aviator sunglasses at the long, lonely stretch of roadway before them. "Your parents are great."

He meant it. They were awesome. They were the family he didn't have, after his own had been snatched away from him when he was little. And they had taken him in like the son they had always wanted. For his entire life he'd been the guy parents hated. But the Rodgers family had liked him from day one, something that still puzzled him a little...another glitch in the Matrix. Even more weird, he loved hanging out with them, shit talking with her dad, helping him out with stuff around their ranch.

Macy was watching him closely; he could feel her gaze on him. "I know you must miss your own. Especially now that we're talking about having kids."

"I guess."

"You don't talk about them much."

"There isn't much to talk about. Most of what I know about them is from faded memories and what my grandmother told me. Now she's gone, too. My last connection was severed."

"Baby." She reached over to wrap his free hand in hers. "I'm sorry. I won't bring it up if you don't want me to."

He shrugged. "Doesn't hurt, doesn't help...there's a void, I guess. But I have you, and you're my family now. You and all your crazy-ass relatives."

Macy laughed, and he took a moment to glance over and admire the scenery: her long, shiny dark hair falling in lazy waves down her bare arm, the length of smooth naked thigh revealed by her shorts. Would he ever get used to her? He could see himself reflected in her sunglasses, some piece of riffraff who didn't deserve her, but was damn glad he had her.

• • •

When Candace had gone into sudden labor with Lyric while she and Brian were visiting Brian's sister in Dallas, Ghost and Macy had been the ones to go to their house and pack a bag for them. Macy had walked into their newly decorated nursery to find Ghost in there among the mint walls and teal drapes, retrieving the car seat from the corner of the room with the baby's diaper bag slung over one shoulder. Neat stacks of diapers rested under the changing table, stuffed animals lined the shelves just waiting to watch over the new arrival. Seeing him like that, surrounded by those things, had caused her ovaries to damn near explode. Especially when those tattooed biceps flexed as he hauled the baby gear outside. He'd also been wearing her favorite pair of his jeans, the ratty ones that hugged his thighs just right and broke perfectly at his heavy black boots. She would never forget that detail, for some reason.

They had joked about what their future baby's nursery would look like. Ghost was horrified that Brian was cool with pastels; Macy pointed out that Candace wouldn't necessarily let him put up Cannibal Corpse posters.

That had been before they'd gotten married. Before he'd even proposed. But it had made Macy so, so happy, and that image of him surrounded by baby stuff was lingering in her head right now. Jesus, she'd waited so long, and she was more than ready to get this show on the road.

As Macy turned her attention back to the road in front of them, a thump sounded from the back of her Acadia, and the car shimmied on the road. "Did we run over something?" she asked. The side mirror didn't show anything but a long ribbon of roadway in their wake.

"No," Ghost said and veered over to the shoulder. "We have a flat."

Lovely, Macy thought, good memories deflating as fast as their tire. Not even halfway there yet, and the universe was trying to tell her this gig was a terrible mistake. She was trying to block out thoughts like that, given her plans for the trip, but they still crept in from time to time. He sent her a sideways glance when she exhaled a heavy sigh.

"Don't worry about it, babe. I'll have it changed in a few minutes."

Of course he would, but still. "All right."

"Unless you want to do it," he teased as he put the SUV in park and killed the engine.

"I could." She'd been changing flat tires since she learned how to drive. Her daddy had insisted.

"Yeah, I know. Come keep me company, anyway."

She got out, the tall grass off the edge of the shoulder tickling almost to her knees. Green fenced-in pasture rolled as far as the eye could see on either side of the two-lane road, dotted with baled hay and grazing cows. Glancing at her phone before shoving it into her pocket, she saw there was little cell reception out here. And that was exactly why her daddy had always insisted she be able to do a few basic car repairs by herself: so she wouldn't have to rely on strangers of questionable motive.

Like her husband, maybe. Grinning to herself, she watched as Seth popped open the back to get the spare and jack. If she'd been stranded out here alone and defenseless—

she wouldn't be the latter if she was alone, though, another of Dad's lessons—what kind of first impression would a stranger who looked like him have made if he'd come along and offered to help? Hell, she had to admit it to herself: she would've kept a wary eye on him.

The black skull bandanna tied around his shaved head, his full-sleeve tattoos, his bulging biceps...she definitely would have been on her guard, same as she had been the very first time she'd laid eyes on him even in a roomful of people. But she also thought a few full-blown fantasies would have been unfurling inside her head. Things she would never admit to anyone but him.

Macy's mouth had run dry, and she didn't even notice he was looking at her over his sunglasses, one eyebrow cocked up. "What the hell are you grinning about?"

"About how hot you look right now."

Chuckling, he bounced the tire down on the pavement. "By all means, tell me more."

Instead, she asked a question that had sprung into her head. "Have you ever stopped to help a girl stranded on the side of the road before?"

"Actually yeah. Afraid I was gonna get pepper sprayed the entire time. Or shot."

Macy laughed and swooped her hair up into a quick, loose bun with the ponytail holder she pulled from her wrist. It wasn't glaringly hot yet, but neither was it comfortable standing out here on the pavement. A fine sheen of sweat was already beginning to collect on her skin. "Why? Were you not gentlemanly?" she teased.

"Oh, I was extra gentlemanly, to ensure that I didn't get shot."

"Was this before we met?"

"Yeah."

"Did you think about fucking her?"

He pushed his shades to the top of his head and stared at her as if he'd never seen her before. "Is this a trap?"

"Maybe." Lightly, she trailed a finger down the spaghetti strap of her black cami. He watched its progression, his predatory gaze caressing the curve of her breast. Suddenly her clothes felt tighter, abrasive. A clear indication she would want to take them off soon.

Understanding dawned in his dark eyes, and he gave a lecherous laugh. She loved that his hands still worked as he spoke to and looked at her; he could do this stuff blindfolded. "You wanna play this out, then?"

It didn't matter that they'd role played dozens of times. The mere thought brought a flush creeping up her cheeks that had nothing to do with the sun beating down on her flesh, and everything to do with the fact that even before devouring him with her eyes just now, she was horny as hell. She swallowed, her throat suddenly parched, and she could swear he watched her muscles constrict. He watched everything, even the bead of sweat that trickled down her chest to soak into the fabric of her cami. Her nipples peaked against the chafing fabric of her bra.

"Fuck, you are a work of art," he muttered, and she lost her breath.

"Thank you so much for stopping to change my tire," she said brightly, striving for the chipper relief of a stranded damsel. "I don't know what I would have done. I would pay you something, but I don't have any money on me."

"No problem," he said gruffly, staring directly at her mouth in a way that told her he had a few things in mind. She loved that he was always just enough of himself when they did this, keeping enough of his own personality to keep her anchored. Because *he* was what turned her on most, not any character he assumed.

While he watched in rapt attention, she swept her tongue

slowly across her bottom lip. Then she turned and walked back to the open passenger side door, feeling the tremble in her knees. She did perfectly mundane things—getting a sip of water from her Yeti, checking her phone for what messages the meager service out here would allow her—while she waited for him to finish his task.

It seemed to take for-fucking-ever, but she knew he did that on purpose. Building the anticipation.

At long last, a shadow loomed over her, and she looked up at him from her seat, making a show of gasping at his sudden appearance as he blocked out the sun. He trapped her, one hand grasping the open car door, the elbow of his other arm resting on the side of the car. She became all too aware of the length of bare leg she was showing him. Aware because he didn't miss an inch with those intense eyes.

"All done?" she asked, plucking a little self-consciously at the hem of her shorts for his benefit. This must be how a mouse felt staring up at a great dark bird of prey. Her heart beat excitement through her veins. God, she was wet.

"I'm just getting started," he said.

"What took you so long?" She let a little snooty-bitch aggravation creep into her voice. Oh, the punishment she imagined that would get her. The smirk he gave her told her he was looking forward to it, too.

"I would think you'd be a little more grateful. I would think you'd be down on your fucking knees."

Oh. Shit. "I'm grateful," she protested.

"Care to show me?"

"Um…" Macy swept her gaze around at their surroundings. A whole lot of nothing stretched in all directions. Still, a few cars had passed by while he'd changed the tire—it was still a state highway, even if it was in the middle of nowhere. She looked back up at him. "What did you have in mind?"

He reached for her. With the knuckle of his index finger,

he trailed a path down her cheek to the corner of her lips. "This pretty mouth wrapped around my dick, for starters."

She struggled for exactly how she might react to a situation like this and came up short…except for maybe going for the concealed handgun in her glove box. That's what made this so thrilling with him, though; she could be whoever she wanted to be. She knew he saw how she melted completely away at his touch. Meeting his gaze directly, she said, "Why should I?"

"Because you want it."

"Well, that's not a good enough reason."

"That's the only reason. You know I can give it to you better than whatever lame dick you have waiting back home." He often liked imagining he was cuckolding some poor imaginary dude in her life. She suspected it was a bit of psychological revenge on his brother, who'd stolen a girl he loved away from him many years ago. Macy never protested. There was no reason to. If he liked it, if he needed it, and if she could help him with it and have fun all at the same time, she was all for it. Even if it wasn't who she was at all, she would be lying if she said it didn't kick an extra surge of adrenaline through her body.

"You don't know what I have waiting back home," she said defiantly.

"I know what you can have right here." He plucked the phone from her limp hand, tossed it to the driver's seat, then dragged her fingers to his cock, hard and straining against his fly.

"Jesus," she muttered, not at all in character. They'd been married for months. They'd been together for far longer. She still marveled at him. And before she even knew it, she was reaching under the hem of his black T-shirt, tearing at his belt and his buttons, and freeing his thick, heavy length from his jeans right there on the side of the highway.

Macy didn't care. Everything, everything about him went straight to her senses and blinded, deafened, and deadened her to everything else in the world but him. Only him. The feel of him in her grip, at once velvety and rock hard. The musk of his need for her, the ragged intake of his breath. The silver glint of the piercing that she knew sought out the deepest places in her and devastated them.

All that was missing was the taste of his flesh, and she didn't deny herself a moment longer, running her tongue along the underside of him. Always her favorite place to start, always seemed to get the most explosive reaction out of him. He didn't disappoint her with the strangled growl that tore from his throat. She closed her eyes as his fist clenched around her hair, demolishing her bun before gently taking it down. That was something else that melted her. His need always tempered with consideration and concern for her. Macy rewarded him with those long sweeps of her tongue that made him shudder, the swirling motions that nearly made his knees give out, the teasing licks around his piercing that made his head fall back, his chest heave. All in preparation for when she at last wrapped her lips around his head, wrapped her hand around his base, and consumed him.

"Oh fuck," he breathed as she swallowed him down as far as she could. He gathered her hair together loosely in his fist, keeping a tenuous grip on control. "Your mouth was fucking made for me, baby."

Every inch of him was made for her. She tried to show him with every move, every whimper. Her fingers found his hips and gripped him hard. With his free hand, he skimmed his fingertips up her bare thigh, and she wriggled her legs wider to accommodate his touch, needing it, aching for it. But he eluded her most greedy parts and suddenly pulled her head back.

She glared up at him balefully, incensed at being torn away

from her task. Instead of letting her get back to it, he reached between their bodies to plunge his hand into her cami and fondle her breast, circling her nipple with maddening strokes so that it stood in a sensitive peak. Her eyes closed again, her breath coming in pants.

"I want to see these," he said, those strong fingers still in her hair as he tore her top down. "I want to suck these." She gasped, praying she wouldn't hear the fabric rip for a split second but then thinking, *Fuck it, I have a dozen*. His sudden onslaught forced her farther back into the car as his lips closed around her nipple and proceeded to destroy every last remaining rational thought she might have. His hands, the wet heat of his mouth, the sharp suction of it, were all that remained. "Want to fuck you," he rasped between hot, sucking kisses.

"Please, oh God, please," she moaned, her hands skittering over his head, his broad shoulders, tugging at him, pulling him in.

"Get in the back."

She almost laughed, but she was beyond it. Always cars with them. Who could complain? From somewhere, she managed to gather the muscle strength to obey him and climb in the back. He followed and closed the door behind him, shutting out the singing birds and distant lowing of the cows. In here it was hot, and she was already sweaty, but when he settled in one of the second-row captain's chairs and pulled her over him, it didn't matter anymore. She couldn't help him get her shorts off fast enough, but she left on her panties. He liked to fuck her with them on.

And she knew, as she pulled her panties aside and he guided the head of his cock to her drenched pussy, that she wasn't going to last a minute. When she lowered herself, stretching around him, her mouth falling open, that became an indisputable certainty. Not one single minute. He felt too fucking good.

Her cry rent the still air; his answering groan vibrated through it. So tight, so perfect, she felt them throb together as they joined, separate pulses beating for each other. In the cramped space, it was uncomfortable, it was difficult, but they had never liked things easy. He rained kisses and caresses across her breasts, letting her have control of the pace. Macy rocked her hips in slow, wide circles, watching his dark eyes when she could see them. Seeing his pleasure, the heavy-lidded rapture there, amped up her own. God, she wanted it to last, but she felt herself tightening already, and it was too good to stop. Every stroke lit a new spark inside.

He knew that, though, damn him. He kissed her mouth and grabbed her hips with an iron grip, stilling her motions while she squirmed and mewled against his lips. "Easy, baby," he murmured between delectable sweeps of his tongue into her mouth. "You'll be done before you've started."

"I've started," she panted.

"I haven't. Not yet."

Jesus Christ. She'd married Superman. "But someone might—"

"Someone won't."

He'd better be right about that, or she might beat him up. If a curious passerby stopped to offer them aid, and she was cruelly denied this building orgasm—and denied *his*—yes, she could possibly resort to violence. "I need it," she whimpered pleadingly, grabbing him by fistfuls of his shirt, rocking her hips as much as she was able. She'd all but forgotten her character, but she slipped back into it in one final, desperate push to drive him over the edge. "Please give it to me. Show me everything I've been missing. Make me come so hard that I'll beg you to take me with you so I don't ever have to go back home."

The iron grip moved from her hips to her ass cheeks as

he growled and attacked her neck, sucking hard at a patch of her skin until it tingled and burned. He took over from there, lifting and impaling her so hard and fast their bodies slapped together, and all she could do was throw her head back and ride and let sensation reign. All those new sparks roared into a conflagration she couldn't battle even if she wanted to, and she let it consume her as she went boneless with the force of her climax. Seth caught her against him, slowing and lengthening his strokes to give her the reprieve she needed while she shuddered and clenched around him.

She could always break him down.

"So fucking wet," he whispered in her ear. "I'm curious to know just how many times I can make this sweet pussy come all over me."

Oh God, he could always break her down, too. And he could probably make her come until her heart burst from it.

"Turn around," he ordered.

"I can't move," she whispered into the softness of his hoodie.

"Move, or I'll move you," he menaced.

He would; he could throw her around like a rag doll. She enjoyed it sometimes. She loved knowing he was strong and had the ability. But the bite of his fingertips into her over-sensitive flesh right now would be too much. So she managed to rouse her heavy limbs into motion and lift herself away from him, immediately missing the hot press of him against her. She shimmied out of her panties before settling on him again, facing forward, leaning back on his hard chest while— *oh God*—his fingertips found her clit and drew tantalizing circles around it.

"I told you," he said into her ear, the rasp of his voice raising the fine hairs there and at her nape. "I told you not to come so fast. You left me behind, and now you're spent and I'm not. That's hardly fair, is it?" He eased deeper into her, forcing the breath from her lungs. Then he jerked his knees wider, which jerked her legs wider, giving him all the access that he needed to drive her insane again.

And he was just beginning to move when the unmistakable thump of a closing car door behind them made them both freeze. "Shit!" she cried, jumping off him and snatching up her panties and shorts; thank God her top was still on.

Of course, Seth had the unfortunate task of wrestling his substantial rock-hard cock back into his jeans and actually getting the fly closed, grimacing all the while. A glance out the back windshield showed Macy the sight she'd dreaded: a highway patrolman walking toward their car. While both of them dripped with sweat and reeked of sex. "Shit shit shit! It's a hi-po."

Seth only laughed. "Aww, caught with your panties down, you bad girl. Get your sweet ass in the front so I can move." He gave her a smack on said ass for good measure, and she squeaked before leaping up into the passenger seat and trying in vain to do something with her sex-tousled hair. Seth, wincing with every move, managed to maneuver himself into the driver's seat just as the officer stepped up to the window. "Cops fucking hate me," he grumbled, then dutifully rolled it down.

"Good afternoon, sir," he said with a formality that almost made Macy giggle, especially considering his previous words. She managed to restrain herself.

"Is everything all right?"

"Fine. We had a flat, but I just got it fixed. We were about to be on our way."

The patrolman glanced from Seth to Macy, who gave him a trembling smile. She was trying damn hard to act normal, but it was difficult when she was still in the throes of her wild sexual heat. While her damned husband was turning in an Oscar-worthy performance, calm, cool and collected, his wrist draped casually across the steering wheel.

"Any reason why you're still sitting here?" Oh fuck. He knew exactly why they were still sitting here.

"Yeah, sorry about that. We were having a discussion." Seth said. *A discussion.* Macy looked down at her hands, pulling her lips between her teeth, willing her expression to remain neutral. "We'll move along."

"I'll need to see some ID first."

He identified them both, questioned them both—Macy assumed to make sure she wasn't in any danger, which kind of pissed her off—and let them go at last. By then, any remnants of her desire were long dead, her first seduction attempt horribly thwarted.

"Hey, at least *you* got off," Seth teased once they were back on the road, reaching over to tickle her behind the neck. "I could still break rocks over here."

"Sorry," she said dismally. "That might have put me off road sex for a while."

"Aw, hell. Don't say *that*. You have to live dangerously every once in a while."

"Yeah, but...how embarrassing."

"Nah. If we were teenagers and they called your parents, now *that* would be embarrassing."

Macy couldn't help but chuckle. "Can you imagine my daddy getting that phone call?"

"I might arrange a trip out of the country."

"You and me both." Her dad had almost caught her and Jared in a compromising position once, but of course Seth wouldn't want to hear about that. Her parents still loved Jared, too, but they would probably like him a lot less if they knew some of the things Macy knew.

Seth fidgeted uncomfortably, and suddenly she felt bad for him despite her newly made rule. "Poor baby," she cooed, running her hand up his densely inked arm. "I bet I could be persuaded into fixing it for you."

To her astonishment, he shook his head. "I'll save it up for you, darlin'," he said huskily, grabbing her hand and giving the back of it a kiss. "Get ready."

A shiver of delight skittered through her. That sounded like it would be well worth waiting for.

Chapter Six

Bad memories swamped Macy as soon as the building came into view. She hadn't remembered exactly what it looked like, but as soon as she'd seen it, she *knew*. That was where everything had almost come crashing down. And even though she hadn't been here in two years, it felt like yesterday when she and Brian had pulled into this parking lot with the intention of surprising Ghost. Macy had gotten the surprise instead when she found him backstage with Raina.

Now she was here again, a similar crowd all around. But Candace was at her side, at least. Her anchor. In the Slaughter's set was starting in twenty minutes or so, and Macy's nerves were jumping as if *she* were the one going on stage.

"Why do you think he likes this?" Macy asked her friend as they lounged near the bar, watching the milling audience. Piercings, tattoos, and multicolored hair were all on display.

"What, performing live?" Candace asked. She looked adorable, her own pink-streaked blond locks in a sloppy updo. She wore ripped jeans and a tiny fitted T-shirt that showcased her own ink, having taken far more advantage of her tattoo artist husband than Macy had of hers. "Probably for the same reason you like to ride horses around barrels as fast as you can."

Macy had to chuckle. Sometimes before a big race, she felt like she was going to throw up. When Ghost had left her to go backstage an hour or so ago, though, he hadn't seemed affected at all. "I don't know," she told Candace. "I mean, I'm competitive. That's a *race*, and I want to win."

"Maybe it's the same for him. He needs to feel he's won over the crowd."

Maybe. It was just one of the inherent differences between them that would never be bridged, she supposed. And that was fine; it was good for them to have interests outside of each other. Sometimes she feared they burned so bright and hot together they would eventually burn out. It was her worst nightmare. So, yeah, this was healthy. At least she tried to tell herself that, as she watched a guy walk by with tattoos all over his face.

"I'm really trying to assimilate," she told Candace.

Her friend chuckled, then waved to Brian, who was headed their way after conversing with a few people across the room. Macy had learned the first time they'd come here that Brian somehow had as many friends here as at home, and that some of these people actually made the long drive to Dermamania just for him or Ghost to tattoo them. Amazing, really, that they were so well-known. It gave her sense of pride to know that she wore Ghost's art on her own skin, but she hated that it was always covered by her shirt. Something so beautiful didn't deserve to be covered all the time, and she wished she had more opportunities to show it off.

"You're here," Candace said. "So I know you're trying to assimilate. And you're doing great. I know he appreciates it."

Brian reached them, and Macy gave him an absent smile.

"You girls look way too thoughtful," he remarked, then leaned over the bar to signal the bartender.

"Macy's feeling out of place," Candace told him, giving Macy a wink.

"I've had like five different dudes ask who the babe talking to Candace is," he said.

"Are you serious?"

"Yep. Absolute shock when I told them. Most of them were like 'How'd he manage *that*?'"

Well. That made her upset on his behalf. Because he'd managed it pretty damn easily. She'd been putty in his hands from the start.

"They're just talking shit," Brian assured her after studying her expression for a moment. "Probably a little terrified I'd tell him they were asking about you."

She had to laugh at that. Good. She was about to say so, but the crowd parted and she caught a glimpse of a face that killed the words in her throat. Grabbing Candace by the arm, she yanked her friend close and spoke directly into her ear. "Look ahead, a little to the left, and tell me you don't see what I just saw. Please."

Frowning, Candace craned her neck, having to stand on tiptoe since she was shorter. Macy watched Candace's blue eyes wander over the crowd, lock, and then widen. Her hand flew to her mouth, then she pulled Brian closer so she could speak into his ear in turn.

Brian, who had been taking a pull from the beer the bartender had just passed him, nearly spat it out when he saw where Candace was pointing.

It was the only confirmation Macy needed. Her eyes had not deceived her.

Raina was in the building.

But it wasn't the Raina that Macy remembered, though she could never forget that sneering face after their confrontation outside of Mezzanine Music back home. The confrontation that had pretty much run Raina out of town. Gone were the long multicolored dreadlocks. In their place was a simple, dark, pretty cut that just brushed her bare shoulders. Gone was the dramatic black eye makeup. Instead the stage lights caught on a soft, masterfully applied natural look. In fact, gone was the sneering expression; at the moment, Raina stood with a group of friends, laughing wildly at something.

She looked…

Damn. She looked *great*. The girl had always been model beautiful, but now she looked practically *wholesome* on top of it.

But she was still here. Macy didn't doubt it was because she knew Ghost would be, too.

Glancing over at her friends, Macy caught both Brian and Candace staring worriedly at her. Brian averted his eyes to the stage, but Candace leaned closer. "Are you okay?"

"What do I have to be worried about? Honestly?"

"Nothing, of course, but…a shock is a shock."

"I'm really not all that shocked. Not that I wanted to see her. I'm simply not surprised."

"Yeah," Candace said, sounding annoyingly unconvinced. She surveyed the crowd for another moment, her lips pursed. "You want to know what I think?"

"That she altered her style to what she thinks he's attracted to now?"

Candace laughed. "You're scarily intuitive at times."

"It doesn't take much intuition. I know how she operates. Do you think she knows he married me?"

"I have no idea." Candace tugged Brian away from the conversation he was having with the Mohawk-sporting guy next to him and asked him something. He shrugged and said something in return. Candace turned back to Macy. "Brian says he doesn't know either. I really think she dropped from the face of the earth for a while after you sent her running."

Macy took a long, *long* drink from her beer. She was going to need it. On the other hand, though…maybe she didn't. Alcohol and outrage were never a good combination. "Apparently she didn't drop far enough."

"Sorry, girl," Candace said. "It'll be fine. We're just here for Ghost. Ignore her."

Easier said than done, especially recalling what had happened backstage in this very venue, what Macy had walked in on. Raina had found Seth semiconscious and hurting after a terrible fight with Macy, after the death of his grandmother, when he thought he'd lost everything, and the girl had damn near succeeded in fucking him in his drunken stupor.

At least…Macy hoped that was the full story. It made sense. She didn't think he would lie to her at such a crucial point in their relationship. Honestly, it wouldn't change anything now even if she found out otherwise; he was hers, and she was his. Their future was together, and she didn't doubt *that* for a moment.

But these were memories she didn't want to revisit, the very thing she'd warned him about when he first brought this idea up to her. These were feelings she didn't want invading their happy place. From the very beginning, she'd told him the whole fighting-over-a-man thing was something she'd left behind in middle school. He'd made her do exactly that, though: fight for him. She wasn't about to do it again, not when he already belonged to her.

Taking a deep breath, she tried to cool the anger brewing in the pit of her stomach. It was ridiculous. It didn't belong.

She needed to see him.

Candace and Brian followed her when she asked them to, and the bouncer let them backstage—the same guy who'd let Macy and Brian back the night the shit had hit the fan. She remembered every moment of that night as if it were branded on the inside of her forehead, a dark scar that would last until the day she died.

"Why are you even mad?" Candace asked as they entered the dim area that reeked of stale beer and weed. "And don't deny it, you are *seething*."

Macy wouldn't trade Candace for the world, but sometimes it kind of sucked having a lifelong best friend who knew everything you were thinking without you having to say a word. Macy could fool a lot of people, and had in her lifetime, but she couldn't fool Candace. "Because I *told* him this would happen."

"So surely you were prepared for the possibility? Isn't that what you just said out there, or was I hearing things?"

"I know what I said," she shot back.

"Mace," Brian said, obviously trying to deflect a tiff between them. "Don't worry about it."

Macy scanned the faces milling about and spied her husband, black-clad and sinisterly gorgeous. She charged straight toward him, interrupting his conversation with Gus. "I need to tell you something."

He gave her a long look, then raised an eyebrow at Candace's and Brian's concerned faces beyond her. "All right. We only have a few minutes. Come on." She let him lead her into a room—thank God, not the one in which she'd caught him with Raina—and waited until he shut the door and turned to face her. Good. She needed to see his face.

"She's here. I saw her."

Like a hawk, she watched him for anything that might be of concern, any flicker of *anything* but anger or disgust. He didn't show much emotion at all, which she supposed was just as well. In fact, he seemed to be waiting for her to go on, but when she didn't, he gave a small shake of his head as if to clear it. "Okay. So? Macy, you're the only one who gives a shit about this."

"You haven't seen her yet."

"I don't care to, either. What the fuck is the big deal?"

"I thought I'd warn you in case you notice her from the stage and completely forget what you're doing."

"Why would I do that?"

"Because she looks incredible. Absolutely I-hate-the-bitch-and-want-to-slap-her fucking incredible."

She couldn't believe it; he burst out *laughing*. "I'm sorry, but that was funny."

"I'm serious, Seth! If I see you up there, and you see her, and you have even the most remote expression of surprise on your face, I swear to God I'm going to charge through the crowd and pull her out by her fucking perfect hair. Because that is *exactly* what she wants, to trip you up. So please don't fall for it."

"Goddamn, I love you like this."

"I told you, didn't I? I knew she would be here."

"Macy." He stepped closer, clasping both her hands in his. He brought her left one up between them, so she could plainly see her wedding ring. A lovely, antique set that had once belonged to his grandmother. From the first moment he'd slid it onto her finger, it fit her as if it had been made for her, just like he did.

"See that? I gave this to *you*. That means *your* face is the only one that might trip me up onstage. The only one I might see and completely forget what the fuck I'm supposed to be playing, the only one that would stop me in my tracks and make me think, holy shit, that belongs to me. The most beautiful face in the entire room, and the only one I'll be looking for. It's been that way since the first time you walked in the shop, and don't you ever fucking forget it."

She drew a deep, cleansing breath while everything about him soothed her soul, from the adoration written plainly in his dark, dark brown eyes to the intensity of his words. "I love you," she said, when nothing else would quite do.

He released her hands to lift both of his to her face, holding her gently while he leaned down to kiss her. "You're my fucking world. My heart beats for you. Only you." He searched her face, her eyes, in that devouring way he had that made her feel as if no stone was left unturned in her soul when he was seeking what he needed from her. "Tell me you believe it."

"I believe it," she said, gazing up at him. And she absolutely did.

Seth's mouth tilted up on one side, a sinfully sexy smirk that made her think of doing very bad things to him. "Well. Just in case you have a single doubt, as soon as we get the fuck out of here, I'll spend the rest of the night showing you." He pulled her into his arms, and she went so willingly, sinking into him. But nothing had prepared her for the flood of heat when he whispered, "We still have a baby to make," next to her ear.

Chapter Seven

Brian and Candace, waiting outside, looked visibly relieved when Macy and Ghost emerged from the room holding hands.

"Dude, I thought we were going to have to take her outside before there was a murder on the floor," Brian told Ghost while Candace laughed. Macy couldn't exactly deny it, so she kept her mouth shut, though she did send Brian a narrow look.

Ghost chuckled. "She's easy to defuse if you know how."

"I'm glad you've figured it out," Candace said, "because after more than twenty years, I never have."

"You lack the proper equipment," Ghost cracked, and the three of them laughed while Macy playfully smacked her husband on the arm.

"Her equipment is just the way I like it," Brian said, tugging Candace closer. No matter how much time had passed, Candace still lit up when Brian touched her. How could Macy be worried about anything when they were all so lucky to have found each other?

Her mushy thoughts were rudely interrupted, though,

by a sudden bellow that erupted down the hallway. "Ghost! Man, are we doing this or what?"

"Coming," he called back, then cupped Macy's cheek, his words for her only. "I'll look for you. And *only* you." His eyes flickered to his best friend. "Watch out for her."

"I will. I'll get her up front so you can see her," Brian promised.

Oh God. She had a sudden image of being in a claustrophobic press of writhing bodies, being pushed and kicked and punched and jostled, getting overheated, feeling faint...this was so not her idea of a good time. But it wasn't for very long, and then they could get out of here and work on much more pleasant things. It was almost over, and the worst had already happened. Hopefully.

Outside, the crowd had pressed close to the stage in anticipation. True to his word, Brian took Candace with one arm and Macy with the other, navigating them around sweaty, intoxicated bodies, bumping past couples making out, herding them through until Macy looked up and was surprised to see the stage directly in front of her. Candace nestled beside her while Brian stood guard behind them, a wall of aggression no one was getting around. Up here, Macy couldn't see the crowd; she didn't have the ability to keep an eye on her mortal enemy.

But she supposed there was no reason to. She could do her best to let it go and watch her husband perform.

Wild appreciation went up from the audience when the guys took the stage, and Macy felt a spark of pride and emotion she hadn't anticipated as she watched her husband prowl his area only fifteen feet or so in front of her, his long fingers hypnotic as they coaxed music from his low-slung guitar.

Eat your heart out, Raina, she couldn't help but think. *Those fingers will be on* me *tonight*.

It was at once strange and euphoric. It was like seeing a secret only she knew broadcast to a club full of people. Of course, many of the people here had probably seen him on the stage before—only Macy hadn't. She was privy to his private performances, when it was just the two of them and his guitar. From the very first night she'd spent at his house, he'd often played and sang for her. She loved it, and she could almost be jealous of everyone else in this room for getting to witness it, too. But hearing their appreciation nearly made her eyes well up. And she couldn't do that here, she *could not*. Certainly it was an unwritten rule somewhere that there was no crying at a live metal gig.

He played his heart out, he hammed it up, he ripped through a monster solo, he sent her winks. Occasionally he sauntered up to the mic and bellowed backing vocals with a snarl that made her contemplate crawling on the stage and attacking him right there in front of everyone. Four songs into a single show, and she was a drooling groupie for her own husband. It was awesome. She found herself whistling and cheering and jumping up and down with Candace at her side.

Why the hell hadn't she done this before?

Well, in all fairness, she'd tried once. It hadn't worked out, and then he'd quit the band. She'd never had an opportunity until now, and she'd tried to talk him out of it.

She'd tried to make it all about her. Her problems. Her feelings.

But this…right now, he had to be experiencing what she felt after a phenomenal barrel race, like Candace had said. The power, the euphoria, the adrenaline. He'd never attempted to deny her that high. She knew in that moment that she could never deny him this, either. Not over her silly hang-ups. If he still wanted to do this, she would have to let him.

What that meant for her dreams of family and quiet nights at home, she wasn't sure, but they would figure it out. There was no reason they couldn't have both, have it all.

By the time the set wrapped up, she was half deaf with ringing ears and the beginnings of a headache, but she was too amped to notice. Brian grabbed her and Candace by the hands and propelled them both through the boisterous audience toward the backstage area. Raina was no longer even a blip on Macy's radar, so naturally, as they were threading through the dense crowd, she suddenly found herself face-to-face with the girl.

Shock flared wide in Raina's gunmetal gray eyes—obviously she hadn't forgotten Macy's face, either. *Keep going*, she thought, *ignore her.* But her feet wouldn't carry her forward; they remained planted in place even as Brian tried to tug her away. Candace looked on in alarm.

This woman had tormented Ghost. Macy could only imagine the sort of toxic relationship he'd endured with her. But when he'd finally broken out, she'd manipulated him with threats of suicide, she'd tried to sabotage his relationships, harass his friends, intimidate Macy, and generally made herself a nuisance. And now she was here, most likely knowing he would be, too.

All of that turmoil, wrapped up in the petite, demure-looking package in front of her at this very moment. It didn't seem possible. Raina recovered her composure, giving an almost imperceptible nod.

"Mace, come on," Brian urged. But Macy remained frozen to the spot, her mind racing, nothing coming from her mouth.

"I'm glad," Raina said suddenly, and Macy couldn't have been more shocked at those words if the girl had slapped her. "I'm glad he's happy. And I could tell he is. It worried me a little, at first, when I saw he was back."

You certainly managed to make him miserable enough. But somehow her words managed to crack the ice around Macy's tongue. "Then why are you here?"

"My husband is old friends with Mark." Raina gestured to the stage. "The singer."

Macy nearly choked. Husband? "Oh...well..." What the hell to say? Congratulations? The poor bastard? "That's... good."

"You look great, Raina," Candace put in, ever the friendly peacemaker, even though Raina had never had nice things to say about her, either.

"Thanks. Yeah, I've made some changes." She looked cautiously back to Macy. "Look, I was a mess, and I never expected to see either of you again, but for what it's worth, I'm sorry about all that. I've moved on. I'm happy." She gestured over by the stage, where a tall, long-haired guy was speaking to one of the security guards. He was handsome and oddly distinguished looking, at least for this crowd. "That's Chris over there. We got married last year."

"So did Seth and I," Macy said. "October."

Raina declined to comment on that. "And we just found out last week we're expecting."

For the second time in less than three minutes, Macy thought she was going to choke. Or vomit. She noticed the bottle Raina turned nervously in her hands: water. No alcohol.

"Congratulations," Candace trilled, bailing Macy out yet again when she felt like she was about to bypass vomiting and burst into tears. "Our son is one now. He's a handful. We managed to get a night out—"

The conversation faded out. Macy just wanted to get away. She didn't even know what was wrong; shouldn't it be a relief that Raina was finally out of their lives for good? A few times, especially close to their wedding, Macy had almost expected her to pop up somewhere like a ghastly jack-in-the-box out of a horror movie, leap out from behind some bushes, or maybe crash the wedding to shriek her reasons why these two should not be joined. All this time, and those fears had been unfounded.

And Raina was pregnant. That was a good thing, but Macy wasn't, and she couldn't fight the tiny gnaw of jealousy in her chest.

She looked to Brian helplessly, since Candace was still chattering about Lyric, and Raina was politely attentive. Two mothers bonding. Macy couldn't take hearing any more. Brian met her eyes over Candace's blond head, understanding dawning in his expression.

"Babe, we need to go," he told his wife. In the past he had definitely turned out to be Macy's ally in many, many ways, and this was one such moment she'd be permanently indebted to him for.

"Well, good luck," Raina said to them, then to Macy, "and you, too." Not waiting for the reply Macy couldn't conjure anyway, she slid away to join her husband by the stage.

She tore her gaze away from the woman's retreating figure just in time to see Ghost emerge from backstage into the crowd, receiving a round of applause from the people closest to the door.

Macy's field of vision narrowed to him and him alone. She made a beeline for him.

Chapter Eight

It had felt fucking amazing being up there again. Better than ever. Knowing Macy was watching had breathed new life into his performance, and he'd seen the pride in her eyes whenever the stage lights caught in them just right. She had actually appeared to be having a good time. He couldn't have asked for more.

Macy practically threw herself into his arms as he emerged into the crowd. Catching her, he laughed as he said, "Hey, hey. You'll have to wait your turn, miss."

"My ass I will." She laced her fingers behind his neck and pulled him down for a kiss so hot and deep and hard that he felt fucking branded right there in front of everyone. And he liked it, but it wasn't like his normally reserved wife. What the fuck had happened in the eight or ten minutes since the set ended? Searching her face once she finally released him revealed nothing but wicked satisfaction.

Something clicked in his brain. Raina. Of course. He'd been having so much fun, he'd almost forgotten that she was even here. Because it didn't matter. But if something had happened, it must have gone well, and he loved that Macy didn't mind claiming what was hers in front of everyone.

"Are you ready to get out of here?" she asked, searching his eyes intently.

"I was thinking I might have a beer or two with the guys. Give me half an hour."

Her lips pursed in an adorable pout he didn't think she ever realized she did. "I know how your half-hours work. They turn into one hour. Then three. Then daylight."

He laughed, keeping his arm around her shoulders as he turned her toward the bar. "Thirty minutes. *Maybe* forty-five. You have my word. I just really want to celebrate."

"Fair enough, as long as you remember the celebration you have waiting back at the hotel room."

Shiiiit. His cock gave a celebratory twitch at the very thought. "Maybe I didn't think this through."

She laughed, putting both her arms around his waist as she shuffled along at his side. "Celebrate with your friends. It's okay. I'll hang out with Candace for a little while longer. Maybe I'll come around and act like I don't know you. We'll see how well you do with picking me up."

He stopped dead in his tracks and turned to face her, not releasing her because he fucking couldn't. Not in that moment. Not with her looking up at him with those molten hazel eyes, pulling him in. Irresistible. "Hell," he managed to croak before swooping in to kiss her, his hand fisted in her hair. "I've changed my mind," he murmured against the softness of her lips. "Let's go."

The tremor that went through her...he felt it in his bones. "Are you sure?"

"Fuck yes." He took another taste of her. She was more intoxicating than anything they served at the bar. "Need you more."

"I'm glad to hear it," she said teasingly. And then she

killed him, right there in front of everyone, when she moved her lips to brush against his ear. "Fuck, I'm horny for you."

Dead. Slain. Done. They said their goodbyes to their friends, and he thought they might not even make it to the hotel. He thought *he* might not make it, because Macy kissed his neck and rubbed his cock through his jeans the entire way. Ghost hadn't come in his pants since he was a fucking teenager, and he wasn't about to start now, but goddamn, she knew how to touch him, even with the barrier between their flesh. He was in agony as they spoke with the desk clerk to check in at the hotel, with Macy beside him all bright-eyed and pink cheeked. All he could think about was another set of cheeks he'd like to see flushed pink. And soon.

The walk was agony. He didn't dare touch her during the brief elevator ride, or he might not have been able to stop. And to not touch her, he had to not look at her right then. Her perfection. Even though he felt her looking at him.

"Is something the matter?" she asked, sounding way too innocent.

"Just waiting until we get to the room," he said casually, letting his gaze rest on the floor buttons, "before I fuck you into oblivion."

"Oh, is that what you think?" She could have been asking if he thought it would rain tomorrow. Slowly, she flipped the key card through her deft fingers. That, he couldn't help but watch. "I'm not sure you can handle what I've got for you tonight."

"I'm sure I can."

"Hmm. I'm not convinced. You've been building up all day. Then you did the show, and I know that took a lot of energy. You must be tired."

"Nothing's better after coming offstage than pussy."

Her mouth dropped open in mock outrage, because she knew by now that if she baited him, he was ready at a moment's notice to return the favor. He let a nonchalant smile spread across his face.

"Really. I take it you've had a lot of pussy after coming offstage, then."

"Never yours, though. It'll be interesting to see if it's as wild with my wife."

The doors opened, and only then did he look at her face. Yep. It was full of challenge. "Oooh. You're treading hard," she said.

"That ain't all I'm about to do hard." He swept his arm ahead to indicate she should walk out ahead of him. Her feet remained planted to the floor of the elevator.

"Oh yeah? You ought to be worried, considering I just had a run-in with your ex. Wasn't hers the *pussy* you dove in after coming offstage?"

The very mention of Raina was damn near boner death, but he laughed, stepping forward to keep the elevator doors from closing on them. Shit, if he took this too far, he might be sleeping in the car tonight. "It's all a blur."

"That's fabulous. All a blur. A drunken blur of pussy!"

Naturally, a couple took that moment to appear in front of them as she bellowed at him, and the look on her face when she was caught made him nearly piss himself laughing. "Sorry," he told the stern-faced man and woman, reaching and grabbing Macy's arm, tugging her forward. "She's had a few too many, you know. Gonna put her right to bed." *And fuck her brains out.*

"Oh my God," she muttered over and over as he dragged her to their room, while the hallway seemed to get longer and longer the farther they walked. "I can't believe I just said that in front of them. Oh my God."

"Can't take you anywhere, you foul-mouthed heathen, yelling about pussy in front of those nice people."

"Well! It's your fault, getting me so riled up."

"So mad about my drunken blur, even though you *know* damn good and well that I much prefer a clear, sober view of yours, baby." She grinned a little at that, so maybe he'd averted the nuclear crisis that had been building. He went on. "Could have been worse. If I'd done what I've been wanting to do since we stepped into the elevator, they might have caught you with more than dirty words in your mouth."

Macy's tongue peeked out to wet her lips. Christ. Their room came into view. Ghost grabbed the key card from her fingers and inserted it. The little green light flashed their success, and then they were inside the dark room lit only faintly by Austin city lights beyond the windows. He could make out the path to the bed, but then the door closed behind them and they were plunged into near-blackness.

Macy gave a lovely gasp as he planted her back against the nearest wall, pressing his mouth hard to hers and tasting her deeply. She shuddered against him in the dark, and he couldn't see her face even with his eyes open, but with that one sensory deprivation came a sweeter flavor in her kiss, a hungrier touch. Her little whimper rent the silence as her fists clutched at his shirt, tugging at him desperately.

His dick hadn't lost the interest she'd aroused in the car and the elevator. Not in the least. When her hands went to his fly to wrench his jeans open and release him, rock solid and straining, so much relief flooded him that he had to pull away from her and groan. Her soft hands went to immediate work, stroking, soothing, teasing, torturing. Fuck. He had to get in her *now*, get the edge off, but she hit her knees in front of him and took him into the loving wet cavern of her mouth. His own knees nearly buckled, his hands shooting out to slam against the wall and keep him standing as she dampened him with her clever tongue and took him deep enough to make his toes curl in his boots.

Once he was certain of his ability to remain upright, he plunged both hands into her silky hair, feeling every movement of her head just before he felt the delectable results on his cock. He ached, and cursed, and fought with himself, and finally pushed her gently away though it took every shred of self-control he possessed.

"Up," he commanded, and she was quick to obey. Her shirt came off in his hands, quickly joined on the floor by her bra, the lace sensual against his fingers but nothing compared to her warm skin. Now that his eyes had adjusted to the darkness, he could barely make out the outlines of her face and body. It was hot this way, but it wouldn't do, not now, not for him. He needed to see her when he loved her. Watch her face, her pleasure, the love in her eyes.

Macy stripped her shorts and panties off and went to work on his clothes, divesting him of everything with an excitingly desperate efficiency. He lifted her in his arms; her legs went automatically around his waist. He carried her to the bed and laid her down before reaching over to fumble for a switch and turning on a single lamp.

Light bathed her gloriously naked body, and she stole his breath as she always did. Her hazel eyes took in his every move as he crawled onto the bed with her, watchful and anticipating.

"You're so beautiful I don't know what to do with you sometimes," he told her, sliding a hand up one smooth naked thigh. She trembled beneath his touch, but kept her legs together. That was fine; he would have a hell of a lot of fun coaxing them apart.

"I really did love watching you tonight," she said, the words surprising him.

"Yeah?"

She nodded.

"I thought it looked like you were enjoying yourself, but I didn't know if you were doing it for my benefit."

A coy little smile curled her lips. "Oh, you know me

better than that."

True. Macy wasn't one to show things she didn't feel. Most of the time. "I'm glad you had fun."

"So, do you think…that's something you would like to do again?"

He paused, surveying her shuttered expression with the distinct and disturbing feeling that his answer would determine whether he gained entry to the closed gate in front of him. Oh, she was paying him back for the elevator, surely. "Why are you asking me that now, huh?"

A shrug of her slim shoulders. "Curious."

"I had a good time," he said, "but no. I don't need it. If they asked me to do it again, I would decline."

"Why?"

"Like I said, I don't need it. It was laid out as a onetime thing and it will remain a onetime thing."

"You wouldn't only be declining on my account?"

One corner of his mouth tugged up in a grin he couldn't quite suppress. Her skin was still tantalizingly soft underneath his fingertips as he caressed it. "No. Why?"

"You looked like you belonged up there. Like you missed it so much, and I realized how I'd made everything about me. How wrong that was of me. I'm sorry."

Such sincerity rang in her words that he was taken aback. Maybe she wasn't trying to punish him after all. Always so hard to read, his Macy, and even after all this time, he often got it wrong, not knowing what was going on behind those pretty eyes until she chose to let him in on it. One of the many, many things he loved about her…the enigma of her. Solving her puzzles. Enough to keep him intrigued for the rest of his life.

"It's okay," he said, feeling at a loss. "Nothing you need to apologize for."

"I felt I needed to."

"I appreciate it. Now, if I don't get to fuck you soon, I

can't be held responsible if I start crying and begging. Can we hold off on the heavy conversation until after?"

She giggled, and finally, *finally,* her legs fell apart in front of him. There might come a day when the sight of her hidden slice of heaven didn't set his pulse pounding and his dick painfully throbbing, but it was not this day. Oh no, this day wasn't it. And fuck that anyway, because that day would never come.

He leaned in to tease little kisses up her inner thighs, watching her reactions, studying the increasing pace at which her breasts rose and fell. Ghost might not always know what was going on inside her mind, but reading her body was an art he had perfected. She mewled with restless abandon, rolling her head on the mattress while he allowed his fingertips and lips to playfully roam free over her soft planes and curves, taking his time even though there wasn't much left before the whole crying thing would set in. But it was only when Macy's legs couldn't get any wider from her need that he settled between them and locked gazes with her as he locked their bodies together.

This was why he needed to see her. The breathless acceptance and trust and need as she took him inside. As colossal as the pleasure was, it was only eclipsed by the love. Who needed drugs, who needed alcohol, who the fuck needed the stage, when they could have this?

"You're so beautiful," he told her, smoothing the hair back from her forehead as he began to move. All games forgotten. Games had their place, they added their spice. But this was everything. *She* was everything. Her mouth found his, her kiss sweet and greedy, her body moving in perfect sync with his.

And ordinarily he would let it last, let it build until the absolute breaking point, but goddamn, he'd left that point way back on the road to get here. When she'd been so hot and wild riding him in the backseat, and they'd been interrupted.

She wrapped him so tightly now, took him so deeply, all his thoughts fractured. He had to come or go insane.

He uttered her name on a growl, shoving his arms beneath her to hug her close. She crossed her ankles behind his back, draped her own arms around his neck, and silently dared him with her body to try and break free. To even entertain the thought of escape was insanity, though. She had him, and she knew it, and he knew it, and it was fucking okay.

"Yes, baby, come for me," she whispered in his ear, and he was a goner, release jolting down his spine and out his body like lightning. Pouring into her wet heat as he thrust deep and held, giving her every drop she needed, his fingertips biting into her skin as her own clenched on his back. Just as the peak of his bliss was letting him down, hers lifted her up, tiny flutters rippling along his cock as she thrust against him and moaned into his mouth.

"Oh my God," she murmured as she shuddered beneath him. "Seth, oh, Seth…"

Sweetest music he'd ever made in his life.

She came hard and long, surprising him for the short amount of time he'd spent inside her. But he wasn't complaining. Especially when she sank her teeth into his shoulder. He always loved that. "Damn, baby girl, you weren't lying."

"Huh? When?" she asked breathlessly, still giving little bursts of shuddering pleasure beneath him.

"Horny as fuck."

"Oh." She managed a sound that started out as a laugh and ended as sigh. "Yeah."

He was well enough acquainted with female biology and timing by now that he pretty much knew what that meant… They might have a major life change nine months from now. It was all good. Ghost gathered his wife into his arms and held her, thinking he would never get close enough. But he would damn sure keep trying.

Chapter Nine

Macy let him have his recovery time while they talked and laughed and rehydrated. Then she took him on a long, slow ride that lasted until she collapsed over him in an exhausted, trembling heap, her sweat mingling with his as he held her and stroked her damp hair. Even as she contemplated sleep right there on top of him, she knew from the spark deep in her belly every time he moved inside her that she wasn't done with him yet.

"Jesus," he groaned in her ear an hour later, "you're gonna kill me, but I'll die happy."

Macy giggled and licked her dry lips. They lay with her back to his front, her leg tossed back over his hip, because neither of them had strength enough to move any more than that position required. "Sleep," she agreed, wiggling free of him before turning and grabbing a drink of water off the nightstand. Once he had a drink himself, she settled on his chest, and he drew the covers up around them.

She was absolutely spent, and more content than she could remember being in a long time. Peace suffused her, but it was fragile, and there were still some things she had wanted to say before hormones had clouded her mind. Macy knew if she didn't say them now, the moment would pass. She would never say them in the morning once the events of the night were a fading memory in the light of day.

She drew a path on his chest, tracing lines of his ink lightly with her fingertips. "I know you don't want to talk about Raina, but she told me something I thought was... interesting."

His chest rose and fell with his sigh. "All right, what?"

"She's married," Macy told him, carefully waiting for any reaction. "She's pregnant."

"Well, good for her."

Relief went through her. She wasn't sure what kind of reaction she'd been waiting for from him, but *virtually none* was the best one he could've possibly given her. "I thought so. She seemed...better. Much better."

"I knew something had to be going on with her. It would take more than a new hairstyle to change her, and I'm still not convinced it's possible. She has it in her to be a good person, though. I've seen it. I saw how happy it made her when she got pregnant before."

With him. "I'm jealous of her," Macy admitted softly.

"Fucking hell, *why*?"

She lifted her head and looked him in the eyes, because she needed to *see* how he reacted to this, needed to know that he was with her, really with her. For some reason, the words came simply, as if these hours with him had removed the cobwebs from her mind and heart so that she could see clearly again. "Because however badly it ended, she still had something of yours that I've never had."

"Baby," he murmured, stroking her cheek as the incredulousness in his eyes softened. "I love you so much. And that's something of mine you have that she never did."

"I know." She dropped a kiss on his chest. "I guess I'm being selfish. I want everything."

"I like when you're selfish over me. And I'll give you everything I possibly can. That's all I want to do, Mace, every damn day. Plus, you know...maybe I did it tonight."

"Maybe," she said, settling her cheek back on his warm skin and lacing her fingers through his. The thought brought a smile to her face, sent a little flutter of excitement through her stomach.

"She shouldn't even be a factor," he told her, sounding the slightest bit troubled.

"I realize that. I don't even think I knew she was a factor until I saw her tonight. I guess she was kind of a loose end floating out there. I always wondered in the back of my mind what she was doing, where she was, and sometimes I felt some guilt over her. Can't help it."

With his free hand, he tickled her behind her neck, while she cringed and giggled and fought him. "Answer me this. If we did it tonight, if we made the kid, or whenever we finally do it, will you chill out? I mean, is that everything? Or will there be something else you need?"

Once she finally subdued him beneath her, his wrists pinned harmlessly at his sides even though he could break her grip with a twitch, she grinned down at him. "Baby number two, maybe."

"Oh, Jesus. I'm not your fucking stud horse, woman."

Macy nibbled at the tip of his nose. "Yes, you are," she drawled. "My big, strong, virile—"

"Maybe you ought to see how baby number one goes before you start thinking about baby number two, yeah?"

"My grandmother had twins. My aunt had twins. Maybe we'll have babies one *and* two."

Pure horror dawned in his expression, and Macy tossed her head back and laughed.

"Are you trying to give me a heart attack?" he asked. "You should have disclosed this information before I signed on. I want out." Teasingly, he made a move as if to get up, but she fought him back into submission beneath her...only because he let her.

"Honestly, *I* would probably have a heart attack if that happened. But you never know, right?"

"Eh."

"Oh, come on, cheer up, you big baby."

"Thought I was your big stud horse."

"Prove it."

He rolled her beneath him so easily a thrill shot down her spine. "Macy, honey, all you would get out of me at this point is a little puff of dust."

She burst out laughing. "You'd better buck up. Start chugging water, or maybe a protein shake. You're all mine for the next two to four days."

"Just let me have some sleep and I'll be good to go."

"Quitter," she teased.

Chapter Ten

Here Macy was again. Every movement precise, she placed the pregnancy test strip on the bathroom counter in front of her and looked up at her reflection in the mirror. But there was one major difference from when she'd been here before. Ghost stood behind her, waiting to see the results with her. And wait they did, the seconds stretching out like years until she couldn't stand it anymore.

"Has it been long enough?" she asked nervously, her gaze flickering up to meet his in the mirror. He stood behind her, arms wrapped around her waist. Both of them had agreed not to look at the results until a couple of minutes had passed, then they would look together.

He lifted his left hand to check his watch. "I think it's been more than enough."

"I'm afraid to look," she said. "Do you think we did it this time?"

Seth grinned, nuzzling her neck. "We damn sure worked at it hard enough."

Macy giggled as his breath and lips tickled her sensitive

skin. "We did, didn't we?"

"And hey, if it didn't happen this time, we'll work at it again. It's not as if we didn't have a good time."

"Okay," she said and took a deep breath. "Are you ready?"

"I don't know. Are you?"

"I don't know." Their gazes remained locked in the mirror.

"You said you've been feeling tired and a little queasy in the morning."

"And I have, I'm just afraid it's wishful thinking. That I want it so bad I'm manifesting it."

"We could always, you know, look and find out."

"But I'll be so disappointed if it's negative."

"Don't be. We have plenty of time."

"I know. But you know me. I'm impatient."

They were silent for a moment. Macy swore she could hear her own pulse in her ears. She could feel his against her back, steady and a little fast. He was nervous, too.

"Ready?" he asked. "On the count of three?"

She closed her eyes. "Okay."

"One. Two…"

All her hopes and dreams centered on this moment.

"Two and a half."

Macy's eyes flew open. "Seth!"

"You're the one who's afraid to look. I'm ready."

"Really? You're totally ready?"

"Absolutely. You're the one being weird about it."

"Then look. And you can tell me. You'll know before I do."

"We're supposed to do it together. Do you really want me to look first?"

"Maybe. I don't know."

"Well hell, let's go all out. Call Candace and Brian over

here. They can look and tell us."

She rolled her eyes. "Now you're being ridiculous."

"We can call your mom and dad, too. They can all come over, and tell us if you're pregnant or not."

"Let's get serious."

"I've been serious. You're the one stalling."

"Okay, Mr. Two-and-a-half. I was ready to look."

"Then look."

"Count again."

"All right. *Three.*"

She gasped, but at the word, her gaze jerked downward of its own accord. So did his. Like ripping off a Band-Aid. They both stared at the test results, the only sound their breathing.

And then all she could do was turn around and collapse against him, feeling his strong arms tighten around her until the breath was chased from her lungs. Even though Macy closed her eyes, the image she'd just seen danced in front of her eyelids as she felt tears well and spill.

That plus sign had stood ten feet tall in the results window.

She was pregnant.

She was *pregnant!*

"Are you okay?" he asked, and she heard the slight tremble in his voice. It killed her in the very best way. But how to explain how she felt right now? Like she was 100 percent changed from who and what she'd been thirty seconds ago, and the enormity of it staggered her. Nothing that used to matter before they'd stepped into this room together mattered anymore, except for him and the life he'd put inside her.

But she had time to tell him all those things. "I am. Are you?"

"Baby, I'm fucking fantastic."

"Promise?"

"I promise."

"Scared?"

"Nah. What's to be scared about?"

Against his chest, she smiled. Of course he would say that. But she felt how his heart rate had kicked up even more, a strong throb beneath the softness of his T-shirt. His fingers slid through her hair as he held her close.

"Do we tell everyone now, or wait a couple of months?" she asked.

"What's wrong with it being our little secret for a while?" He dropped a kiss on the top of her head, and she nodded.

"I like that." Their little secret. She relished the thought of sharing knowing glances with him while they were around their loved ones, giddy with excitement at what they had accomplished while everyone else was in the dark. They would have plenty of time to decide the perfect occasion to let everyone know.

But, God, it was going to be hard to keep this secret! Especially from her best friend who would probably ask right out how things were going in their attempts to conceive.

"Candace will figure it out," Macy said. "There's literally no way she won't."

"You're probably right. And if she knows, so will Brian, and then so will everyone else at the shop."

"And we probably shouldn't tell our friends before we tell our families."

"So what are you thinking?"

"Let's give it a couple of weeks. Then we'll tell them. We probably won't be able to keep it any longer than that."

He scoffed. "You won't make it that long."

Macy gave an exaggerated gasp and lifted her head to look up at him. "You have no confidence in my secret-keeping abilities, do you?"

Seth's eyes crinkled in that adorable way when he smiled. "Nada. I know how you are. You'll blurt it out the first time you see Candace. Admit it."

Okay, he might have a point. She couldn't imagine anything harder than seeing her friends or her mother and not letting them in on this amazing, magical news right away. But she would do her best.

There was another thing she couldn't imagine, either. Standing in this bathroom and discovering these results without Seth by her side, without his arms around her as she learned that their lives were changing forever. He deserved to be a part of this moment, so she would be eternally grateful that things hadn't worked out the last time she'd been in here stressing over a pregnancy test. Things had a way of falling into place, didn't they?

Macy smoothed her hand over the back of Seth's head and marveled, for just a moment, at how far they had come from where they began. And at everything that lay ahead for them, so much that she couldn't wrap her mind around it all yet. But they had almost nine months to get it all done.

It was going to be so much fun.

"Are you happy?" he asked, trailing his lips over her ear and down to her neck.

"I'm the happiest I've ever been in my life." She turned her head to meet him in a kiss. "There's nowhere else on earth I would rather be than here, right now, with you."

"Macy, every moment with you has been that way for me. Every fucking moment." Then his kiss turned hungrier. God, he always managed to start that melting in her chest, that warm glow that spread out until every part of her was heated and trembling for him.

"Guess we'd…better…take advantage of these… spontaneous moments…while we still have them," she said, only managing to push out the words when he let her come up for air.

Macy felt his smile against her lips, then his tongue danced in for another taste. "We'll always have them," he told her. "We'll make them if we have to."

"I think making spontaneous moments defeats the purpose of spontaneity."

"Whatever you want to call it," he growled, cupping her face with both hands. "I love you."

"I love you, too."

She hadn't realized tears were streaming until he used both thumbs to wipe them away. "It's all happening, baby. Everything we wanted."

We. Macy couldn't even begin to tell him how much it meant to her that his dreams matched her own. There had been a time when she doubted, at least a little. She couldn't allow those little insecurities to creep in anymore, not when he showed her every day, with his every breath, with every beat of his heart, how inconsequential they were. How much she meant to him.

"Thank you," she whispered, stroking the side of his face and staring into his eyes. Normally dark and unfathomable, right now they shone. Seth shook his head and opened his mouth, but she moved her hand to lay a finger against his lips. "You've changed a lot for me. I know you're willing to change even more. But I don't need it. I love everything about you. Sometimes I worry about things I don't need to worry about, but you're the one constant in my life, and I need you just that way. Constant. Exactly as you are. Especially now."

He smiled, looking a little puzzled. "I know that."

"Do you really? I don't tell you enough. We disagreed about the band, and I'm afraid it made you doubt me."

"So...you're saying *not* to trade in my GTO for a minivan just yet, right?"

Macy laughed at the hopefulness in his voice. "Hell no. It all began in that car, right? And you say I already have a mom ride. You keep that car from now on if you want. I never get tired of seeing you in it."

"And my job? I mean, I have other ideas of things to do, but I'm happy there, and—"

"What would we *really* do without Dermamania?" It had all begun there as well. The relief in his expression almost pained her. "You do what makes you happy. If you're happy, I'm happy."

"I have to admit it's nice to hear you say it," he said.

"Then I'll say it more."

He shook his head and gently pressed his lips to her forehead. "You're perfect the way you are, love of my life."

"If I didn't know any better, I'd think you were still working toward one of those spontaneous moments."

"You know me well," he murmured, beginning to steer her into the bedroom with a wicked grin. Suddenly, he stopped and scooped her up into his arms before continuing toward the bed. "Better idea. I need to carry you around while I still can, right?"

Macy squealed and broke into laughter, but she couldn't let him get away with that one. "While you still can, huh? Before I get big as a house?" She poked a fingernail into his chest. "Oh, I'm gonna make you pay for that one, Seth Warren."

"Baby, I'm looking forward to it."

• • •

He had never known he could feel this way.

The idea of a baby had been somewhat abstract. The *knowledge* of a baby, of evidence that a life was nestled inside his precious wife, that he'd played a role with her in creating it…it was a life-changer. In that fraction of a second when he'd seen the plus sign, all the petty concerns that plagued him on a daily basis had vanished. Gone. They were nothing compared to this amazing news.

A few years ago, the man he'd been would have felt trapped, freaked out. Actually, he'd been there before and knew exactly how he'd felt. The man he was today had never felt more free. All thanks to the woman in his arms, showing him what was important. He tried with every kiss and every caress to show her how grateful he was as he made love to her.

"You don't have anything to worry about," he told her after, his hand gently caressing her still-flat belly as they both watched, both dreamed about the future. He couldn't wait to see her grow with their baby. "This is everything, Macy. I'll fight like hell to protect you, and this one. I promise. If I've ever made you feel unsure, I'm sorry. I'll do better for you both."

She put her hand on top of his. "I love you so much."

"I didn't have much hope for anything when we first got together, you know. You changed everything for me."

"Sometimes it scares me to think maybe you'd rather things go back to the way they were back then. You were so different, and I worry that you think you made a mistake getting married to me. That I ask too much."

He caught her face in his hand, stroking her cheek. "*Never* think that. I can't even imagine not having you. I wouldn't be able to breathe, baby. You're it for me. If you ever doubt it again, ask me, and I'll tell you, show you, rent billboards to announce it to the world, I don't care. Whatever it takes. Because there is no reason for you to ever feel scared of that. You're the best thing that ever happened to me, and I can't wait for this next journey with you."

Her eyes filled with tears, shining with love. Ordinarily that would undo him, but he knew these were happy tears. "You can really be sweet when you want to be."

"I'll even be sweet *all* the time if you ask me to."

And there was the devilish grin he knew and loved. "Nah. I also like it when you're bad."

He was glad to hear it, because he happened to think they were the perfect mix. Dynamite one minute. Pure tenderness the next, like now. Snuggling her closer, he buried his face in her hair, breathing her in. His very reason for living. He'd never thought he would need nor find another, but with their discovery today, she'd given him that, too.

Maybe he didn't deserve it, Seth thought as his love, his wife, the mother of his child began to doze in his arms. But he would damn sure take it.

About the Author

New York Times and *USA Today* bestselling author Cherrie Lynn has been a CPS caseworker and a juvenile probation officer, but now that she has come to her senses, she writes contemporary and paranormal romance on the steamy side. It's much more fun. She's also an unabashed rock music enthusiast, and loves letting her passion for romance and metal collide on the page.

When she's not writing, you can find her reading, listening to music, or playing with her favorite gadget of the moment. She's also fond of hitting the road with her husband to catch their favorite bands live.

Cherrie lives in East Texas with said husband and their two kids, all of whom are the source of much merriment, mischief, and mayhem. You can visit her at http://www.cherrielynn.com or at the various social networking sites. She loves hearing from readers!

MUFFIN TOP (A BBW ROMANTIC COMEDY)
a *Hartigans* novel by Avery Flynn

The only thing about me that's a size zero is the filter on my mouth. But when some random guy suggests I might not be eating alone if I'd ordered a salad instead of a hamburger I'm shocked silent, which is a feat, trust me. That brings us to one sexy fireman named Frankie Hartigan. He's just apologized for being late for our "date" then glared at the fat-shaming jerk. Next thing I know, he's sitting down and ordering himself dinner. I have no problem telling him I don't need a pity date... unless of course it's to my high school reunion next week. Oops, what do I do now that he's said yes?!

NEVER EXPECTED YOU
a *Love Unexpected* novel by Jody Holford

When Zach Mason, former army sergeant turned veterinarian for war-wounded animals, returns home, the decision to stay is easy. But convincing the only other vet in town to hire him is a good deal harder. It doesn't help that the beautiful, intelligent, and stubborn Stella Lane is determined to make his life hell. Too bad she's nothing but temptation. And now his new roommate...

SCREWED
a novel by Kelly Jamieson

Cash has been in love with his best friend's wife forever. Now Callie and Beau are divorced, but guy code says she's still way off-limits. Cash won't betray his friendship by moving in. Not to mention it could destroy the thriving business he and Beau have worked years to create. But this new Callie isn't taking no for an answer. He's screwed…

NAILED IT
a novel by Cindi Madsen

I'm Ivy Clarke. And I'm in over my head, trying to flip a house all by myself. I'm not too proud to admit I need some help. Too bad the only one who can help me is the same man I want to throw out this house's second-story window. Jackson Gamble and I can't be in the same room together for more than a minute without devolving into a sparring match. Get in. Renovate. Get out. Keep my heart firmly in tact. Because it's much easier to fix up a house than a broken heart.

Made in the USA
Middletown, DE
22 June 2022